"Are you certain y̶o̶u̶
Mercy asked.

Wyatt hopped for̶

She reached up, the̶ ̶ ̶ ̶ ̶ ̶ ̶ ̶ ̶ ̶ ̶ ̶ ̶ ̶ ̶tter of
it, and returned her̶ ̶ ̶ ̶ ̶ ̶her sides. "Thank you.
Personally, I'm not concerned but…"

He smiled. "But your father thinks it is best. I agree
with him. There was something in Robbie's eyes."

"Yes, I saw it the day he came over and ordered me
to court him. I have no interest in being that kind
of a wife."

"No, I suspect not." He grinned.

"I suppose you think a wife should stay in her place
and be told what to do by her husband?"

"No, I didn't say or even mean to imply such a
thing. I know that you would want to be an equal
partner in a marriage."

She relaxed and walked over to him, gently grasping
his shoulder.

He captured her hand with his and kissed the top.
"I'll see you in the morning."

Her cheeks flamed. Perhaps her father had reason to
be concerned about Mercy's honor in his presence.
Father, help me be the man Mercy needs.

Books by Lynn A. Coleman

Love Inspired Heartsong Presents

Courting Holly
Winning the Captain's Heart

LYNN A. COLEMAN

is an award-winning and bestselling author and the founder of the American Christian Fiction Writers organization. She writes fiction full-time and loves visiting places like Savannah and other historical locations. She makes her home in Florida with her husband of thirty-nine years. Together they are blessed with three children and eight grandchildren.

LYNN A. COLEMAN

Winning the Captain's Heart

HEARTSONG
PRESENTS

Recycling programs
for this product may
not exist in your area.

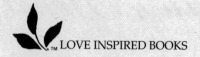

™ LOVE INSPIRED BOOKS

ISBN-13: 978-0-373-48716-5

WINNING THE CAPTAIN'S HEART

But a Samaritan, as he traveled, came where the man was; and when he saw him, he took pity on him. He went to him and bandaged his wounds, pouring on oil and wine. Then he put the man on his own donkey, brought him to an inn and took care of him.

—*Luke* 10:33–34

I'd like to dedicate this book to old friends—
Robin, Susie, Penny and Joyce. We've known
each other since grammar school and we always
have such a good time together when we meet up.
Love you guys so much. Who would have thought,
growing up on Martha's Vineyard, we'd be
getting together in Florida so many years later.

Chapter 1

A groan emanated from the marsh's edge. In the ditch on the side of the road, a heap of clothing caught her eyes. A second groan. Mercy left the handcart in the road and hurried to the ditch. Compassion filled her as she beheld a beaten man, blood covering his face. His right leg lay at an odd angle. "Broken," she murmured. "Are you all right?" She waited for a response. "Of course he's not all right. How ridiculous to even ask," she prattled on. Dawn danced on the horizon as she watched her steps down the ditch to the marshy grasses that made up St. Augustine's inlets.

The man shifted and yelled.

"Stay put. I'll get some help." She ran to her cart, pulled out a clean towel from the folded laundry, as well as a canteen of water. Having made a clear path a moment ago, she could maneuver easily down the slight slope without fear of sliding into the muck. "You've been beaten, I think. You also appear to have a broken leg. Please lie still and I'll help you."

The stranger nodded his head. She dampened the cloth and washed the drying blood from his face. Its coppery scent mingled with the smell of mud. He moved, yelped and passed out. Mercy continued her gentle ministrations. Several wounds were deep and would need sutures. *Should I run to town to fetch the doctor?* On the other hand, was it wise to leave him alone in this condition?

Light footfalls approached. Mercy glanced up and saw young Moses, one of her father's former slave boys. Moses and his family continued to work for her father on the cattle ranch. Moses was around ten and as helpful as any boy could be. He wore no shoes, light blue trousers and a white linen shirt, as many of the sharecroppers did. He was a hardworking boy, who often did what he could to earn a penny here and a penny there. "Miss Mercy, is that you? Whatcha got there?" Moses squatted next to them.

"This man's been beaten and has a broken leg. I can't move him. Moses, run to town and get a doctor."

"Ain't sure I's can do that. Pa says to be right quick comin' and goin' today."

Mercy reached into a small pocket she kept in the waistband of her skirt. She had begun putting these pockets in when she started working in town. A place to hide her money without dragging along a purse seemed practical. She pulled out a silver quarter. "Will this help?"

"Pa won't mind if I's earnin' some money. I's be back faster than the Florida rains."

Mercy looked at the sky. There wasn't a cloud in

sight yet. "Wait, Moses." She pulled out another quarter. "Deliver these linens to Tropical Breezes Inn for me."

"Yes 'em, I's can do that. Pa will be so proud of me."

Mercy smiled. "Bring the cart back and I'll have another quarter for you, too."

"Yes 'em." His big white teeth glistened in the sun.

"Doctor first," she said.

Moses grabbed the handcart and ran toward town. Mercy prayed the laundry would stay clean. It wouldn't do to have her customers upset with her. She'd deal with that later. For now, she had a stranger to tend to. Mercy shifted her attention back to him. He moaned again.

"Do you have family here?" she asked. She'd never seen him before. Although with the blood and swelling on his face, he could be someone she knew and she might not recognize him..

"Nooo," he said, face strained.

Many folks had been moving to Florida since the war's end, five years back. Mercy's father's family had been here for generations. Her mother's family had come from France on their way to New Orleans. Their ship had stopped in the port of St. Augustine, and they'd loved the area enough they decided to stay.

"I've sent for the doctor. Try to relax." Mercy continued to wash his wounds, then waited.

"What happened to you?"

"Robbed," he groaned.

"Oh, dear, I'm sorry. Did you have a horse? Were you walking?" Mercy realized she should have sent Moses to bring back the sheriff, as well. The sound of leather and horse hooves approached. Mercy scanned the road. Moses stood on the back of the dray wagon. The doctor was sitting up front, and another man was driving the team.

"What's the emergency, Miss Hastings?" Dr. Peck asked. Even the good doctor was new to the area. He lived here with his mother and two sisters.

"This gentleman has been robbed and appears to have a broken leg. He's been beaten quite badly."

Dr. Peck climbed down and grabbed his small black valise. Moses jumped out of the wagon. "I's fetched the doctor like you said. I's going back and get your wheelbarrow."

"Thank you, Moses. Can you get the sheriff, too?" Dr. Peck interjected. "Tell him to come to my office. I need to do some work on this poor fellow."

"Yes, sir." Moses ran back toward town.

The gentleman driving the dray wagon stepped down. "Need a hand?" Mercy didn't recognize him. He stood around six feet tall and had broad shoulders and a round belly.

"Yes." The doctor straightened the man's leg, and the patient screamed. "Miss Hastings, hold his leg while I attach these braces. Then Mr. Duncan and I will lift him onto the wagon."

Mercy's hands trembled. She knew he was in tremendous pain, and she didn't want to cause any more.

The doctor covered her hands with his. "Hold the leg this tight."

"Yes, sir."

"Thank you." He quickly bound the man's leg between two thin slabs of wood. "You can release him now, Mercy." She did as instructed. Dr. Peck continued. "All right, on the count of three… One, two, three." The man groaned but didn't say another word. They walked him up the slight bank on the side of the road and raised him onto the flat wagon.

"Thank you, Mercy, I'll take it from here." Dr. Peck

climbed into the bed and squatted beside the injured man. The driver stepped up onto the front seat. He encouraged the horses forward. Slowly, they turned the wagon around and headed for town.

Mercy stood there for a moment, debating what to do. Should she continue on her journey to town and meet Moses with her cart or wait for him? Then again, she still had dirty laundry to pick up from the inn.

Mercy decided to follow the disappearing wagon in front of her. She pulled out her handkerchief and covered her nose from the swirling dust that filled the air. The rainy season hadn't begun yet in Florida, and now, at the tail end of the dry season, everything was parched and brittle. Which was a little odd so close to the ocean.

Mercy scanned the harbor. Ships lined the docks; folks were loading and unloading cargo. St. Augustine seemed alive and vibrant. Mercy's mind drifted to the wounded stranger. He had no family in the area. Where would he stay? How would he recover? She hoped the robbery wouldn't set him back too much. "Father, care for this man and help him heal."

Mercy thought of her own family and how close they were. She loved them dearly and didn't want to part from any of them. Her life on the ranch was good.

"Miss Mercy, come here," Jethro Billings called out as she approached the back of the Tropical Breezes Inn.

Wyatt didn't know a man could experience this much pain and live. The doctor had given him something, and he supposed it helped but honestly couldn't tell. The real pain came in knowing the bandits had gotten away with his life savings. He'd been on his way to purchase a steam yacht. *His* ship. After years and years of squirreling his money away, he'd finally saved enough to buy one, to be captain of his own vessel, in charge of his own life.

The sheriff didn't hold out much hope of finding the money but said he'd be looking into it. The difficulty was Wyatt had been attacked in the evening and hadn't gotten a look at the men or even recognized a voice. Still, the sheriff hoped they would do something foolish and start spending a lot of cash. Wyatt prayed God would help recover the unrecoverable. Why he'd agreed to pay cash rather than giving the owner a bank note as others did, he'd never know. Wyatt squeezed his eyes shut. There was something important in the recesses of his mind he couldn't pull up.

"Mr. Darling," Dr. Peck greeted as he walked into the small room where Wyatt lay on a narrow cot. He reached and touched the plaster cast. "Good. It is hardening well. How do you feel?"

"Miserable."

The doctor smiled. "I completely understand. You should be thankful Miss Hastings came by when she did. Not too much longer and I would have had to cut off your leg because of infection."

Wyatt scanned the long white cast and nodded.

"You should heal well. I was able to set the bones in place without a lot of fuss. I spent a fair amount of time cleansing the wound. I'm hoping you don't get any infection. I'll need to remove the cast and examine it again in a week unless you feel your leg swelling before then.

"Mr. Darling, I heard your exchange with the sheriff. I can let you stay for a couple of days, but after you're on your feet…"

"Thank you, that's very kind, Dr. Peck. I'll be out of your hair as soon as possible." *And on the trail of those who robbed me.* Wyatt looked down at the cast. He wouldn't be mobile for a while and working on a ship would be impossible. *Dear God in heaven, what am I going to do? I have nothing.*

"I'll speak with the Reverend. Perhaps he'll have a suggestion."

"Thank you." What else could he say? For the first time in many years, he was helpless. Someone must have followed him from the bank. But who? He hadn't seen anyone trailing him or even heard anyone. He hadn't gone straight to the wharf, but rather stopped at the inn for a roast-pork dinner with Spanish rice and fresh vegetables. He practically gorged himself on fresh fruits or vegetables whenever he was on shore leave. His stomach rumbled.

"Are you hungry? I can order a late breakfast from Pedro's. He makes a delicious hash, very mild, not spicy. When you're feeling better, you'll want to try his full-breakfast menu. Or I can have my mother or one of my sisters prepare something."

"I'd be beholden, Dr. Peck, because I can't afford anything right now."

"Shh, breakfast is on me. I was heading that way when the boy came for me." Dr. Peck's hand lighted on his shoulder. "Lay down and rest while I get our breakfast."

"Thank you." The thought of not providing for himself didn't set well. He'd been on his own since he was thirteen and a cabin boy on a ship. He worked his way up to first mate and if… He scanned his broken body and let out a deep sigh. *If it hadn't been for this, I'd be the proud owner of my own ship. How could this have happened, Lord? Please, help me find my money.*

The cuts on his face burned. How many men had

attacked him? He'd worn a money belt. No one could have known. Wyatt closed his eyes and conjured up the memory of the beating. He remembered the first punch when he refused to give the men his cash. Were there two or three? He squinted harder, trying to focus. Pain seared his brain, but no further image developed. He relaxed his squinting and tried to think of pleasant things. The ocean. But the realization that he wouldn't own his own vessel trumped the delightful thought of the blue waves crashing on the shore, rolling in and out. *No,* he chided himself, forcing down the unwanted interruption. The gentle to and fro of the surf played again in his mind, lulling him back to a peaceful state.

Once more, the scene was shattered by the jarring memory of his head being beaten, his stomach, back and legs being kicked. He'd fallen to his knees as the beating continued. They hadn't just wanted his money, he realized—they'd wanted his life. Fear sluiced through his backbone, like a gale-force wind slapping a tattered sail.

Wyatt groaned.

"Can I help you, sir?"

He opened his eyes and focused on a middle-aged woman clothed in a light gray dress with red roses embroidered around the collar and cuffs.

"Sir, can I get you something? John said he'd be back shortly."

John? Who was that?

"Pardon me. Dr. Peck said he'd be back shortly. Are you certain you're up for a Spanish breakfast? My sister and I can scarcely manage the mildest of those hot peppers."

Wyatt closed his eyes. "No, thank you. I'm fine," he replied, not sure what he was saying no to.

"Forgive me for saying so, but did you partake in

spirits? No good can come from them." She started cleaning up the area.

Wyatt hoped the good doctor would be back soon so this ever-so-helpful woman could vanish back into the interior of the house. He kept his eyes closed in hopes she'd think he'd fallen back to sleep.

"Open your eyes, sir. Dr. Peck said you must not sleep."

Wyatt opened his eyes. "No, I did not partake."

"Well, you poor soul, getting a beating like that." She shook her head in disbelief. "I don't know what this world is coming to. I lost my fiancé in the war. Nothing has been right since. Here I am, a grown woman past my prime, living with my mother, brother and sister. Do you have any family in the area?"

"No." Did the poor woman know how hard it was to concentrate on her endless chatter?

"I'm sorry to hear that. Do you have family somewhere that I can pen a letter to?"

"No. I lost them while I was a young lad."

"Where are you from?" she asked.

"New England…Cape Cod."

"Mother was born in Connecticut. Father was born in New York, and so were the three of us. We came here after John secured a place for his practice. He felt the warmer climate would be helpful for Mother. She's seventy-nine now. I see by the cut of your cloth you're a sailor. Where have you traveled?"

"Mary, thank you for your assistance," Dr. Peck interjected, reentering the room. "You may help Mother now."

The doctor stepped up to his bed. "I'm sorry about that. I had second thoughts about your resting and the concussion you had, so I asked my sister to help keep you occupied."

"She can..."

Dr. Peck laughed. "Oh, you have no idea. She's a sweetheart. She found love late in life, but her fiancé had the unfortunate lot of passing during the war. Becca, on the other hand, has never been fortunate in love. It seems we Pecks are doomed to a single life. It's not what I pictured for myself while I was a young man. But I've grown accustomed to my life and, to bring a woman into my world now... Well, living with three already, I just don't know if I could handle another."

Wyatt chuckled and groaned. "I'm thirty and pretty set in my ways. Sailors find it easier to remain single. I've all but vowed to remain single myself. Although, captains, on the other hand, seem to have no problem keeping a wife. Of course, they're hardly home, working weeks or months at a time. Maybe that's the secret," he said with a wry smile.

Dr. Peck set a small table beside Wyatt's bed and placed a tray with a cloth covering their meal on it.

"Smells wonderful."

"Good. You'll need the protein to regain your strength. I brought some cornbread, oatmeal and scrambled eggs, as well as some Mexican egg casserole and some chilaquiles."

"Chilaquiles?"

"*Sí,* as Pedro would say. They are tortilla chips, fried and covered with green-chili sauce and cheese. I love them. But they might not agree with you just yet. Your abdomen sustained a few blows. Start with some oatmeal and some tea. Let's see how you handle that."

"All right." Wyatt shifted. Pain drove through his broken leg.

The front door to the doctor's office opened and closed. "Miss Hastings, how may I help you?"

"I came to see how your patient is doing."

Wyatt remembered that voice—so sweet, so obliging. A hazy image of a woman with darkening blond hair and bright blue eyes flooded his memory. His rescuer.

"He's doing fairly well. He just saw stars, I believe, trying to move too soon. Come on in. We were about to eat breakfast."

"Oh, I couldn't impose."

Wyatt smiled. "Thank you for your help, miss." What was it the doctor called her? *Hastings.*

The doctor motioned for her to take his place at the bedside. "Miss Hastings, if you wouldn't mind assisting Mr. Darling with his breakfast, I'd be appreciative. I still haven't had mine, and the hour is approaching for my rounds."

"What would you like me to do?"

"Help him eat. Movement is difficult for him at the moment. He'll be up and about tomorrow."

"With a cast?" Wyatt found his own words echoed by Miss Hastings. She stood about five foot and a half, perhaps an inch less. She seemed to have a slight, pleasing frame concealed well in a billowy outfit.

Dr. Peck chuckled. "Yes, with a cast. I'll find a pair of crutches for you to use. Now, if you two will excuse me, I'll let Mary know I've left you down here. Please call her to stay with Mr. Darling when you have to leave."

Miss Hastings nodded.

Wyatt groaned.

"Are you all right? Can I help you?"

"He's fine, just frustrated by the confinement. Thank you for your assistance, Miss Hastings."

"You're welcome, Dr. Peck."

* * *

Mercy cringed at the sight of the poor man's wounds. He had stitches over his right eye, a stitched gash over his left cheek, and black eyes framed his enlarged, broken nose. Multiple cuts and abrasions covered his bruised and swollen face. She shifted her thoughts away from the injuries and scanned the breakfast table. "My gracious, are you hungry?"

"Yes, very. Doc said to start with the oatmeal. I can't sit up."

Mercy scanned the room. "Give me a moment. Ah, that should do." She walked over to the other bed and grabbed the pillow. She fluffed it and placed it behind Wyatt's head, helping him lift his body as she adjusted the pillow. He felt so alive in her arms. Unlike a couple of hours before.

"Thank you."

"You're welcome. I'm happy to help." She set a chair beside the bed, took the bowl of oatmeal in her left hand and grabbed the spoon with the right. After placing a good-sized portion on the spoon, she fed it to him.

His face flamed.

"I can't imagine how you feel, having to be helped this way, but remember, Dr. Peck said you'll be up tomorrow."

"It's hard to believe it hurts to raise my arms, but they are also badly bruised and cut in several places. Mmm, this is good oatmeal."

"Pedro does a fine job. I recognize his Mexican egg casserole."

"Ah, so you're from here?" He took the next spoonful with much more ease.

Mercy smiled. "Yes. We're one of the few families who have actually lived in Florida for several generations. We aren't the oldest family in the area, but we've been around for a hundred years. Tell me what happened."

"I was ambushed. Three men, I think. I don't know how they knew I had my entire life savings in my money belt. I was supposed to buy my ship today. I'm a sea captain. Well, in name only now."

"I'm so sorry. How long will you stay at the doctor's office?" Mercy continued to fill the spoon with oatmeal and feed her patient. His brown eyes softened when she fed him, but had hardened when he spoke of the robbery. His hair was still matted with dry blood. She wondered if she should wash it for him but thought better not to ask.

"The doctor said possibly a couple days."

"I'll pay for you to have a room at the Tropical Breezes Inn for a week."

Wyatt shut his mouth tight. "No. I can't allow you to do that."

"Oh, nonsense. Of course you can. I have been earning my own keep for years now. The innkeeper, Mr. Billings, and I have a business arrangement. I do their laundry. He'll give me a good price."

"I'll pay you back."

"If you must. But honestly, I feel it is my Christian duty to do this for you."

"Good Samaritan, huh?"

Mercy giggled. "I guess I am. I hadn't thought of it that way. But you were on the side of the road, beaten, robbed and in need of help. So I guess I am your Good Samaritan. Which means you have to accept my help. After all, the good Lord is watching."

Chapter 2

"Mercy, what were you thinking?"

She'd been trying to explain to her parents the events that transpired today. Her father was a good man with a kind heart, though frugal to a fault, in her estimation.

"Papa, please try to understand. All his money was stolen. He was about to buy a ship. His entire life savings were taken from him. The Bible teaches us to look out for one another, like the Good Samaritan. The minute I found him beaten on the side of the road, I knew I had to treat him the way Jesus taught us."

Placated, her father sighed and sat back in his chair.

"You'll be very proud of me, Papa. Mr. Billings gave me a reduced rate. He agreed to half price, once I explained who I was renting the room for."

Her father's smile broadened.

"Isn't that marvelous, Jackson?" her mother piped up. Mother seldom spoke in opposition to her husband in front of the children. Mercy knew that to be different behind closed doors. Over the years, she'd heard her parents argue in private about how to proceed with their children's discipline. But in front of them, they were always united. Rosemarie Hastings was a strong and wise woman, and Mercy respected her mother.

"Yes, very good. I understand why you helped this stranger. And we should pray for the return of his money. You say he was going to purchase his own ship?"

"Yes, Papa. He and the sheriff told me of his loss. I don't have nearly as much money that it would take to purchase a ship saved, but if I were to lose all my savings…" Mercy shook her head. "Can you imagine?"

Her father bowed his balding head. "No, I can't imagine." He raised his gaze. "And his leg is broken?"

"Severely. Dr. Peck is quite concerned. He told me it was possible that his leg might not fully recover. He should be able to walk again, but he will likely have a permanent weakness in his right leg. Can a man who doesn't have sound legs work on a ship?" She remembered stories of sailors with peg legs but thought perhaps that was only in fiction. "Dr. Peck also said that if I hadn't found Wyatt Darling when I did, he would have had to cut off the lower part of his leg. We can be grateful for lower temperatures last night."

"Gracious," her mother spoke up. "Jackson, how can we help this gentleman?"

"I don't know." He rose from his chair. "I need to milk the cows before dinner. Let's all pray about this and see if there is more to do than simply pray." He placed his hand on Mercy's shoulder. "You did right, sweetheart. I'm sorry for questioning you."

"Thank you, Papa." Mercy's heart swelled. His words of approval would never fall on deaf ears. Jackson Hastings wasn't a man who prided himself on giving undue praise, so when he gave it, Mercy's heart soared. She knew she'd done the right thing. Of that, she had no question. But coming up against her father for an act of kindness and spending her own resources to do it, well... Father was strict on budgeting matters. If he hadn't been, Mercy wouldn't have a large savings. She wouldn't be running her own business. Being a laundress was something she could do and do well, and it produced a reasonable income. Living at home with her parents kept her expenses low. All in all, Mercy had a good life.

The swollen face of Wyatt Darling came back to mind. Mercy offered up another prayer.

"Mercy, let's cook some chicken soup for Mr. Darling. You know what my mother always said about chicken soup."

Mercy chuckled. "It's good for the soul and good for the belly."

"That's right. I do miss her."

Grandma Clémence had passed away last winter from consumption. Mother arrived at her mother's home a day too late. Mercy knew it had broken her mother's heart not to speak with her mother one more time before she died. She reached over and gave her mother a hug. "I miss her, too." Grandmother was from France, and consequently, Mercy had been given the English translation of her grandmother's name. She'd also learned to speak and read French, a language that was rare in Florida. Spanish was much more common, apart from English and the Seminole language, although that was rarely spoken after the Seminole wars.

"Go fetch one of the chickens and prepare it for cooking," her mother instructed as they both wiped tears from their eyes.

"Oui, Maman." Mercy left the house and went to the chicken coop. Selecting a chicken was easy. You picked one that was no longer laying eggs. Generally, her father kept them in a separate pen. However, there were none in that pen today. Which meant she had to select one that was still laying eggs. The sacrifice was great and not truly necessary. She hesitated to do it without letting her mother know there wasn't one available. On the other hand, preparing food was her mother's way of helping someone in need.

Decided, Mercy stepped into the pen and chased down a chicken. With one swift twist, she wrung its neck and began preparing the bird for her mother's gift to Wyatt Darling.

Three hours later, her parents were dressed for an evening ride to Dr. Peck's office. Mercy stayed home to make certain evening chores were finished and her younger siblings did schoolwork. She also had a heap of laundry to iron and fold for her clients.

Bessie, her youngest sister, still a towhead, with ring-lets that bounced when she walked, came up to Mercy carrying a slate tablet and a chalkstick. "I don't understand how to do this."

Mercy glanced at the math problem…long division. "Show me where you are having trouble."

"With the whole problem. Why do we need to do math, anyway?" Bessie stomped her foot, and her delicate pink, lower lip pouted. "It's not like we're going to use it once we're married." Bessie was nine and believed the entire world revolved around her.

"Well, for one thing, you need math in order to cook."

"Really? I think you're just trying to get me to learn how to do this."

Mercy chuckled. "Really. For example, let's say I

wanted to make pancakes, but the recipe makes thirty pancakes and it was just my husband and me having breakfast. What would you suggest I do?"

"Give a lot of pancakes to the pigs."

Mercy held down her laughter. "No, you'd divide the recipe to a fourth of what it called for, right?"

"I guess. Do I really have to learn division?"

"I use it all the time in figuring what to charge my customers."

"I don't intend to have a job. I'm going to stay at home like Momma."

"Momma still uses math."

Bessie crossed her arms and pouted again. "All right, show me how."

Mercy went on to explain how to figure out the problem and was pleased to see Bessie finally grasp the concepts. Her multiplication tables were rusty, but given some time, Mercy felt her younger sister would at least get by with her basic math skills. For her part, Mercy loved the subject, at least until it came to algebra. That's where her math skills ended. X equals whatever squared, minus C didn't interest Mercy.

Mercy went back to her ironing. Ben, who was sixteen and nearly six feet tall, came up beside her. He grabbed a towel and started folding. "You had quite an adventure today."

"The poor man."

"I've been thinking about going to medical school, but I don't know if I should leave Papa alone with all the cattle."

"Have you spoken with Papa about this?" Ben was a sensitive young man but very methodical. Even in folding the towels, he made crisp, straight creases.

"Not yet. There is considerable expense involved in

the education. I do well in my science and math classes, and my Latin is graded high enough, but I don't see how we could afford my education."

Mercy placed the iron back on the heating plate. "If the Lord wants you to be a physician, like Luke, then he'll help with the money. The question is, do you have a burning desire to help people in this way? If you noticed, Dr. Peck isn't married. He spends a lot of his days and nights caring for others. Would that appeal to you?"

"Yes, I think so. I was wondering if Dr. Peck or one of the other doctors in town would take me on as an apprentice. I could go to their offices after school and get a real feel for the work they do."

"I think that's a marvelous idea, Ben. Would you want to leave this fall for college?"

"I don't know if I'm ready. I need to speak with my teacher and see if he can school me in the higher math and science classes. Another year's preparation for college might be wise."

Mercy folded the sheet she'd just ironed. Ben worked on the towels. She set the various items in their proper piles. "Ben, I think you're approaching this in a sound manner. Speak with Maman and Papa. Let them know your plans and desires. I'm certain they'll support you on this. As for the ranch, let Jack and Papa worry about that." Jack—Jackson Jr.—was their older brother, who lived on the south end of the ranch. He and his wife were expecting their second child.

"I know you're right. It's just that I'm the only other son, and the ranch is too large for two men to run it."

"As I said, let Papa figure that out. Don't get ahead of yourself. Start by seeing if medicine is the career path for you. Working with open wounds and sewing people back together again might not be what you want." Even as Mercy spoke the words, she knew Ben had the disposition for such labor and that he'd make a fine doctor. "As for the money, God will provide. He always has."

Ben shook his head. "I think about what happened to Mr. Darling and those bandits taking everything he saved for. How was God working there?"

"God obviously wasn't getting through to the men who chose to beat him, but the Lord did have me come upon Mr. Darling in time to save his life and his leg. Money is something that can be replaced. A person's life can't be."

"True. Thanks, Mercy. I love ya." Ben kissed her cheek.

"I love you, too. Now tell Amy and Bessie to get ready for bed. I'll be up to tuck them in soon."

"Sure." Ben, being the only male child left in the house, had a room to himself, whereas Mercy shared her room with her two sisters. Before Jack and his wife, Diane, moved to their own home, Father built a room in the barn and finished it off so that no animal odors penetrated the walls. There was enough room for a bed, chest of drawers and a small sofa. It gave Jack and Diane their own space. Mercy often thought about moving out there herself but had never approached her parents.

She focused on her work and set everything in her cart to be pushed into town in the morning. Images of Wyatt Darling mangled on the side of the road caused her to pause. She shook off the horrific sight and prayed once again for the man's quick and complete recovery.

The generosity of the residents of St. Augustine overwhelmed Wyatt. Throughout the day yesterday, the expressions of warmth and caring went beyond anything he'd experienced before. The sheriff also came by to report he had no news yet. He did ask about his satchel with his clothing and other items. Besides apparel, he had a Bible, a journal, a sextant, and not much else. Sheriff Bower felt he'd be able to capture the men who had stolen his money, if they hadn't left port already.

Wyatt chastised himself again for capitulating to the seller's wishes. He should have known something was amiss. He should have insisted on the owner meeting him at the bank, then the onus would have been on the seller's shoulders and Wyatt wouldn't be in this predicament.

Then again, the owner of the ship was still in town and had told Sheriff Bower he would still sell the boat to Wyatt if he were able to regain his funds. Was the seller behind the theft? Was he trying to get double for the ship? The steam yacht had survived the war and was in good shape for its age. The engines were in very good working order and the current owner, James Earl, kept the sails in fine repair. Wyatt had investigated the ship thoroughly before agreeing to purchase. They even spent the better part of a day out at sea, giving the ship a run for her money. She handled well and would be a good craft if caught in a storm. Unfortunately, at this point in time, Wyatt didn't trust anyone. Not even the sheriff.

Wyatt had been to St. Augustine numerous times over the years, opened a bank account here and had hoped to make it his home port. Now his dreams were gone. Ten years of savings vanished. *Stop it.* He had to start over, all over. And with the pain he was in right now, he wondered if his Good Samaritan should have left him on the side of the road to die. At least then he'd be facing a future he understood.

The beautiful face of his rescuer came to mind, his

own personal Good Samaritan, with her dark blond hair and azure eyes. Even her parents had showed up with a container of chicken soup the first night and told him they were canning the rest and it should be ready for him sometime today. Wyatt scanned the numerous food items left by strangers. For two days, he'd been receiving such gifts. *Father, forgive me for being so angry regarding my loss. Please help me recover the money.*

"Ready?" Dr. Peck came in with his cheery disposition. "I need to see you successfully walk with those crutches before I can release you."

Wyatt didn't know if he wanted to leave the safe confines of the doctor's infirmary. There was security here, and lying in bed at the doctor's office seemed more logical than staying in bed at home. Home? He didn't have one, just a borrowed room, rented by someone else. Wyatt shook off the dread that washed over him as he glanced at the proffered crutches. He pulled them to his side. His hands shook. The weight of the world hung on his arms, compounded by the bruises and cuts they'd sustained.

"Remember," Dr. Peck cautioned, "move the crutches forward, then the left leg. Your upper-body strength will come in handy. Absolutely no pressure on your right leg for six weeks. I want that bone to heal."

"Yes, sir." The doctor had relayed the same instructions last night, the first time he'd tried to walk with the crutches. He'd done horribly and even put too much pressure on this right leg. Pain had shot through his body and he'd fallen to the floor. It was enough to remind him never to do that again. Wyatt placed the crutches on either side of himself and pushed up on the handles while stepping up on his left leg.

"Great! A little more practice and you won't even be thinking about how to raise your body off the bed."

Wyatt didn't know if he wanted to be reminded that walking like a cripple would become second nature to him. Once fully upright, he positioned his body and his right leg to push off with his left and the crutches. He moved forward. "Excellent, Wyatt. Take another step."

Wyatt smiled, then let his smile fade. It hurt too much. "May I see my face?"

"Sure. Just remember, all those wounds will heal. Well, your nose might not be as straight as it once was."

Wyatt didn't consider himself a vain man, but he was partial to the face his parents and the good Lord had given him. The doctor came over with a hand mirror. "I'm sure you've seen your share of men who've been in a brawl. And you know how contusions heal, so don't be too frightened by the image."

"I can handle it, doc." A tiny piece of him wondered if he truly could. The ugly, swollen image in the mirror did not reflect anything he'd seen in the past. "I should not have seen guests. It's a wonder the women didn't run out screaming."

Dr. Peck chuckled. "They all knew it wasn't the real you."

The door to the doctor's office opened. Wyatt turned. Mercy Hastings in all her God-given beauty stood in front of him and smiled. "You're up."

"Marginally."

"That's wonderful. How's he doing, doctor?"

"Overall, pretty well."

"I have the wagon with me. My parent's wanted me to invite you to our home. They felt you might need some help with your medications and food. If you're willing, my brother Ben and I will take you to our house and set you up in a private room in our barn. My brother Jackson and his wife Diane lived there for a year while they built their home. If you prefer to stay in the inn, that is also fine. Whichever you would like."

Wyatt wobbled. Dr. Peck held on to him. "I'm stunned. I don't know what to say."

"Yes is a good response." Mercy smiled. "Mother says you got a taste of her cooking the other night, so you know you'll be well fed."

Wyatt laughed. "Yes, she's a mighty fine cook."

The front door of the doctor's office opened again. This time a strapping young man of about sixteen stepped in. He had the same hair coloring and blue eyes as Mercy. Her brother, he presumed. "Dr. Peck, I have a question for you, if you have a moment."

"Sure, Benjamin. Give me a minute." He turned toward Wyatt. "Are you stable again?"

"Yes, sir," Wyatt answered, feeling the sweat build up on his palms and forehead.

"Good. Miss Hastings, please come beside Mr. Darling and be his spotter. I want to see him walking back and forth a few times before I release him."

Mercy nodded. The doctor went to the backroom with the young man.

"Is he your brother?" Wyatt asked.

"Yes. Are you up for walking?"

Her beauty captivated him. Her kindness warmed him. He closed his eyes and concentrated on the matter at hand. He needed to get well, and he needed to do it yesterday, in order to find out who had stolen his money and destroyed his future. He glanced back into her sea-blue eyes. "I think I can. I'm more concerned with getting up and down. I don't mean to be indelicate. What about the privy?"

"The outhouse is not too far from where you'll be staying."

Wyatt nodded. He wore a pair of the doctor's trousers. The doctor was a little wider around the middle than him, but his own clothing had been tossed out. "Good." Sweat beaded on his upper lip. His ears began to ring. Each beat of his pulse caused his entire body to throb. Weariness surged through Wyatt. "I think I need to sit down."

"Cross the room and sit down in the wooden chair with arms." Miss Hastings pointed. "You can do it."

"Easy for you to say."

"Sure is."

Was she teasing him? He turned and saw the sparkle in her eyes. Or did she like seeing pain in others? No, she was too compassionate for that. The doctor's door opened again. A stranger of Hispanic origin walked in as he fell down on the chair.

"You are Senor Darling, *sí*?"

"*Sí.*"

"*¿Habla español Usted?*"

"*Sí, hablo un poquito.*" Wyatt answered. "*¿Como se llama?*"

"*Me llamo Pedro.* Perhaps we should speak in English for Miss Hastings?" Pedro suggested.

"And I am more comfortable with English. Are you the one who made our breakfast the other day?"

"Yes. Did you like?"

"*Sí, me gusto.* Yes, very much. Pardon, Miss Hastings."

Mercy smiled. "I know enough Spanish to understand what you two said."

Pedro turned to Miss Hastings and smiled. "I've come to offer you free meals at my restaurant, Mr. Darling. I understand you've been robbed. I can help in this small way."

"*Muchas gracias, Senor.* Miss Hastings's family has offered me a room at their home."

"Very good. Mrs. Hastings is a sweet woman. She is a good cook, too. She made our family a very nice dish after my father passed a few years back. When you are in town, you come to Pedro's and I will serve you, no charge. I am heartsick that someone in our city would do such a horrible thing. You come when you can."

"Thank you." Wyatt's heart felt as though it was stuck in his throat. The doctor entered the exterior office with young Benjamin trailing him, smiling from ear to ear.

"Good morning, Pedro. Is everything all right?"

"Fine, fine, doctor. I came to see your patient."

Dr. Peck smiled.

"I must get back to work. It is good to see you, Dr. Peck, Miss Hastings, Master Hastings…and a pleasure to meet you, Senor Darling. I see you soon at my restaurant." As Pedro left the building, a woman carrying a brown satchel came in.

"Mr. Darling, my name is Edith Hutchinson. I've brought some clothing my Henry used to wear. I believe it should fit. The pants might be a little long, but they can be hemmed. There are a couple shirts and…" Edith Hutchinson blushed. She leaned closer and whispered, "…some unmentionables."

Wyatt felt the heat rise on the back of his neck. "Ah, thank you, Mrs. Hutchinson. I don't know what to say."

"I believe the good Lord would have me give you these things. I certainly don't need them. And Henry, God rest his soul, doesn't." She handed him the satchel and reached out her right hand. Wyatt took it and discovered there was something being pushed into his palm. He looked into her brown eyes. She winked. "Take it," she whispered. Wyatt obeyed and slipped his hand in his pocket.

The smile on Mrs. Hutchinson's face brightened her countenance.

Ben and Mercy Hastings loaded up all his gifts onto their buggy.

They smiled at one another as if they were in on the secret. Was his Good Samaritan responsible for this overwhelming display of love from this community? He watched Mercy as she spoke with her brother. The joy in her eyes, the love she showed him, created a deep yearning within Wyatt that he thought was long buried. Sweet memories of his family emerged. And as quickly as they arrived, the black clouds of the past swirled around them and covered the memories in darkness.

He glanced back at Mercy and the darkness dissipated. Was Mercy Hastings his knight in shining armor? No, it was deeper than that. Who was this wonderful creature? At that moment, nothing else mattered. His goal was to find out who she was and what part she would have in his future. Because, as of this moment, Wyatt knew he had a future.

As time passed, Wyatt found himself getting wearier. Perhaps it was too soon to leave.

"Ready to go?" Benjamin asked as the last person offering yet another gift left the doctor's office.

"I believe so. Dr. Peck hasn't shown me how to handle stairs, though."

"That's all right. He gave me instructions." The doctor had left an hour before on house calls. Of all the people who had come into the doctor's office this morning, only one had wanted to see the doctor. And that was the young man standing in front of him now. "Here you go." Benjamin handed him his crutches.

"So, how do I get down the stairs?"

"One foot at a time." Ben laughed.

Wyatt chuckled. "Great, we've got a comic in the house."

"Seriously, you use one crutch and the other hand on the handrail. You use the crutch as if it were your right leg. Then jump down one step at a time."

"So the doc really did tell you how to use these?"

"Yes, sir. Plus, I used them last year when I sprained my ankle. I didn't have a plaster cast, but I did have to stay off my foot for a while."

"No better teacher than someone who's experienced the same pain. Lead on, Master Hastings."

Mercy stood at the bottom of the steps. Strands of hair stuck out of her bonnet, dancing in the wind. Her sea-blue eyes sparkled. Again, he asked himself, who was this incredible woman? And why was he so fortunate to have his path cross with hers?

Chapter 3

"How are you feeling today, Mr. Darling?" A week had passed since he had come to stay with Mercy and her family. Ben was now working with Dr. Peck and Mr. Darling was under Ben's oversight. At first he didn't seem to mind Benjamin's overenthusiasm, but as time wore on, Mercy could see Mr. Darling's patience waning.

Mercy stirred the oatmeal into the muffin batter. She glanced up and admired the healing in Wyatt Darling's face. At first it had been so swollen one didn't have any idea what he truly looked like. Now he displayed dual colors of green and purple under a crown of brown hair, along with ragged strips of black sutures tied together. "Did you sleep any better last night?"

"Some. Thank you." He maneuvered around the chair and sat down at the table. "I was wondering if I could ride into town today? I'd like to speak with the sheriff and see if he's been able to find any leads."

She still had a hard time fathoming exactly how much Wyatt Darling lost that night. "I'll check with Father, but I don't believe he needs to use the wagon today."

"Thank you. I appreciate everything you and your family have done for me. It's a bit overwhelming at times."

"I understand. And you know we're more than happy to help in any way we can." She couldn't imagine how hard it would be to live in a strange town and on the kindness of others. Many of the residents of St. Augustine had come together to help Wyatt Darling. She'd never been as proud of her church as she had been this past week as they responded to Rev. Cotton's plea for this injured man. Mr. Darling now claimed to have more clothing than he'd ever had in his life. Financial gifts came his way, which enabled him to insist on paying for his food. He ate precious little, but Dr. Peck explained that was common with someone who'd had so much trauma done to his body.

What the doctor couldn't explain was this attraction to a stranger that Mercy felt. At first she chalked it up to the emotional flush involved in rescuing him. Now she wasn't quite so certain. Every time she saw him hobble to and fro, her pulse fluttered. And yet he was still a stranger. He spoke little about himself or of what had happened to him.

"Mr. Darling," she said and paused.

"Call me Wyatt."

"Only in private. Father and Mother would not approve of such intimate address in public."

"Very well. In private, call me Wyatt." He placed his crutches on the floor, within arm's reach but out of the pathway of others. Settled at the table, she poured him a cup of black coffee, just the way he liked it, and placed it on the table in front of him.

"Wyatt, tell me of your family. Where did you grow up?"

"I grew up on the sea. I started as a cabin boy when I was thirteen. My family hails from Cape Cod, Massachusetts, a small seacoast town called Cotuit Port. Many of the young men I grew up with went to sea much younger than I."

"Are your parents still alive?" Mercy thought he'd said something before about having no family, but that seemed rather odd. Perhaps he only meant that he had no family here in St. Augustine.

"No." He paused and reached for his crutches. "Forgive me, Miss Hastings, I don't mean to be rude, but there are some things that are personal."

"I'm sorry. Forgive me for being so forward. I'll bring your coffee and breakfast out to your room in a moment."

He stood and adjusted his aids under his arms. "Thank you." His voice was horse, raspy even. Perhaps she should have kept her curiosity to herself. Mercy went to the outdoor kitchen and fried up some eggs and bacon for Mr. Darling.

She'd already been to town today. Mr. Billings needed the linens early this morning. She didn't want to tell Mr. Darling she had no need to go again, but she didn't want to lie to him, either. She could use the time to settle some of her accounts. A couple of her customers hadn't paid when she had delivered earlier this week. These men would honor their debt, of that she had no doubt. But it would give her good cause to go, without Mr. Darling being aware that he was imposing on the family.

If she'd learned anything about having this stranger

in her home, it was that somehow God was asking her to sacrifice her time, her money—whatever it took—to be of service to Mr. Darling. With the little piece of his past revealed, she wondered what had happened to his parents and the rest of his family. *How could one man have so many tragedies in his life?*

His breakfast done, she plated the food and headed toward the barn. As she entered the building, she saw his door partially drawn. She froze. On his back was a wide, ragged scar, traversing from his right shoulder to the left side of his waist. *Dear Lord, what has happened to this man?*

"Mercy?" Wyatt grabbed his shirt. "Forgive me." Turning quickly, he lost his balance. She ran to his aid and stabilized him before he fell on his backside. His breakfast didn't fare as well and landed on the floor.

"Thank you," he said, gasping.

"Please tell me that scar is not from your family."

"No, it is not. I had a kind father and mother."

Mercy's shoulders relaxed. "Sit. I'll bring you some more breakfast." She gathered the fallen plate and left his room.

"Thank you," he said as she hustled back out the door. He wondered if he should explain the mark on his back but hesitated. There were parts of his past that were too brutal for the likes of such a kind and tender-hearted girl. Correction, Mercy Hastings wasn't a girl in any way, shape or form. She was a woman who stirred foolish thoughts. He hopped to the chair, sat down and waited for Mercy's return.

While he waited, his mind drifted back to the attack last week. He could remember the pain, some of the hits but few of the words his attackers had said.

The incident was still a blur. "Father, help me remember," he prayed.

"Here you go." Mercy returned and placed the plate on his lap. "If you'll excuse me, I'll track down Father and ask to use the wagon."

"Thank you, again." Wyatt grabbed his fork and concentrated on the mouthwatering food rather than the most beautiful pink lips he'd seen in his life. "If you're busy, I'll ask Ben to accompany me."

"No, I have some business in town. Ben is at school today."

"Ah, I could use some more book learning myself. I do all right, but a man should know more than basic math and writing if he wants to keep good logs for his ship."

"I…" She hesitated. "I'll be back soon." Mercy turned and exited the room faster than she had come to his aid.

Perhaps it's time to find another place to live. He certainly didn't need temptation in his life, especially when it was taking every ounce of his strength not to track down his attackers. He mentally followed the sound as Mercy rode off on one of the horses.

Jackson Hastings was a Florida cracker. His ranch boasted five hundred head of cattle and a few workers. He relied on the help of his sons, family and a couple of sharecroppers, as far as Wyatt could see. Borrowing a wagon to go into town could put a certain strain on the ranch. Wyatt should have asked last night rather than coming up with the idea this morning, after he had slept in.

For the past week he'd learned all about Benjamin Hastings's dream to become a doctor one day. Wyatt hoped he showed enough patience with the boy, but his constant attention was as disconcerting as a squall in the distance on the ocean. Which was one of the reasons for asking Mercy and not Benjamin to take him to town. That too was probably a mistake. At least with Ben he knew he wouldn't face temptation—if you didn't count wanting to muzzle the boy for ten minutes. Truthfully, he couldn't blame him for being excited about his career choice. He remembered the day he'd decided to become more than just another deckhand.

Wyatt's mind drifted back to the swells of an ocean voyage long ago. He was sixteen and enjoying the beauty of the tropical islands, the crystal blue seas and the dolphins swimming alongside the ship. He sat in the bow and dreamed. He wanted to be free, as free as the dolphins, without a care in the world. Then a large shark swam toward the dolphins, its dorsal fin sluicing through the water. He marveled at how the pod of dolphins fought together to protect each other.

Captain Nickerson had come up and sat down beside him. "They're amazing creatures, aren't they?"

"Yes, sir."

"Wyatt, I know you've been suffering with the loss of your family. But I think it is high time you look at your life and decide what it is you would like to do with it. By that, I mean you decide on your education, boy. Do you want to go back to your home and run a farm? Do you want to stay on the sea? If so, do you want to be a crew member or do you want more for your life? Furthermore, what would your parents expect from you? If you decide on a future, let me know. A boy like you with such a fine mind should be educated. Far more than you received in grade school."

Wyatt opened his mouth to respond, then closed it. He didn't know what to say. "Thank you, sir. I'll think about it."

"Do one better, son. Pray about it." Captain Nickerson stood up and squeezed Wyatt on the shoulder. Wyatt glanced back at the dolphins.

Life would be easy if he were a dolphin. Then he thought about the captain and his protection over the last two years, fighting off the sharks that circled around him when it came time to go to shore or after he received his pay. Everyone was out to have him gamble it away or spend it foolishly. Captain Nickerson had taught him the value of a dollar.

They had sailed into St. Augustine the next day and Wyatt opened his first savings account. Captain Nickerson also helped Wyatt with his family assets helping him find a caretaker and rent out the property he inherited after his parents' death. The land had lain idle for three years.

His thoughts drifted back to the present. Was God trying to tell him to change his future, to work the land and not the sea? Had this loss been God's way of preventing him from making a wrong choice for his future? And he must have some assets from the collected rent all these years, something he never thought about but left in Captain Nickerson's oversight.

Wyatt grabbed a pen and paper and wrote a letter to Captain Nickerson, telling him what had happened and asking his old mentor to help him decide what to do now.

Twenty minutes later, his letter was penned and Mercy knocked on the door frame to his room. "Wyatt, I've loaded up the wagon. Are you ready?"

"In a minute. Could you seal this letter for me? I don't have any sealing wax."

"Be glad to. I'll meet you at the wagon."

Once he made it to the wagon, he found Mercy climbing up her side. "Need a hand?"

"No, thank you. I can manage."

"Remember not to put any weight on the right leg."

"Yes, nurse."

Mercy pursed her lips and handed him the sealed letter. He slipped it in his shirt pocket.

"Sorry, I didn't mean to sound so sour. I'm unsettled and I shouldn't be taking it out on you."

She nodded.

He'd hurt her. He climbed on board, pulled up his crutches. "I can drive, if you'd like."

She handed him the reins. Wyatt felt the soft leather in his bare hands. How long had it been since he'd driven a wagon? Life at sea was certainly different than life on land. "Mercy," he whispered, "I truly am sorry."

"I know," she whispered in return. "Father is watching. You better get a move on."

Wyatt cracked the reins. "Yah," he yelled. The horse lurched forward, then steadied his pace. "Sorry."

Mercy giggled. "How long has it been?"

"Five years. After I became first mate, I had little need to transport anything on or off the ship. I oversaw the deliveries, the men and the supplies, along with making sure all the captain's orders were carried out."

"I love sailing. I've been on a steamboat a couple of times to travel to Palatka, but the few cruises I took on board a ship in the open ocean... Well, I really enjoyed the feel and the sounds."

"I prefer sail. But steam is changing the speed at which our cargo can travel to port." He'd spent a lot of hours debating whether to buy a steamboat or a sloop. Each had its advantages. So he had decided on one that was both, a steam yacht.

The urge to itch his leg under the cast took his mind from his conversation with Mercy. He wiggled his leg trying to make the cast scratch the unreachable spot.

"Are you all right?"

"Just a—confound it—an itch! Doc said I'd be having urges like that."

"That's good. It's a sign of healing."

"Healing is good. But I want to shove a stick down there and scratch." Wyatt tried concentrating on the road. The ocean view opened before him. He could recognize a couple of ships in the harbor.

"Perhaps we should stop by Dr. Peck's office and see if he needs to change the cast. He mentioned wanting to do that at some point."

Wyatt turned his gaze away from the harbor to Mercy. "Perhaps, you're right. Although I don't know if we have time for a new cast to harden."

"We can always ask. If he wants to change it, you can return tomorrow if it needs more time to dry. You can park the wagon outside of the doctor's office, and I'll do my errands in town. Would you like me to mail your letter?"

Wyatt handed the letter over to Mercy. "Thank you. I'll be at the sheriff's after I speak with the doctor." He parked the wagon and Mercy climbed out. She nodded and walked down the street toward the old fort. She was dressed in a pale green dress with a small bow tied neatly at the back of her waist. Wyatt turned his gaze to the doctor's office. He didn't have time for imagining things that could never be.

Mercy walked toward Opal's Inn to settle their account. Leaving the wagon at the doctor's office was easier than maneuvering it through the narrow streets of the old section of the city.

Wyatt Darling knew how to twist a girl's heart. She was falling in love with him bit by bit. The tiniest of comments about his past or his life compelled her to want to know more about him. She also suspected her parents were aware of her growing attraction. She recalled the way Father hesitated in letting her drive the wagon to town. Which, it turned out, Wyatt could manage for himself. He loved sailing. She loved sailing. He loved his parents, even though he didn't talk about them. She loved her parents and could talk all day about them. They had a lot in common. There was ease in conversation with him that she'd never enjoyed with another individual.

She didn't want to jump to conclusions, but he certainly could become her spouse. She had never met a man that held her interest, apart from her father, and he didn't count. There was so much she didn't know about Wyatt Darling, yet every fiber of her being wanted to know everything about him. She fought herself constantly not to ask too many questions.

Then the memory of the scar on his back came into focus. She stumbled on the walkway. "Are you all right, miss?" A man dressed in black steadied her elbow.

"Yes, thank you. I must not have been watching where I was going and my heel caught on one of the bricks."

"You be careful, miss." He tipped his top hat. "Have a nice day."

"Thank you again." She paid more attention to her feet and the placement of the brick pathway as she continued on her errands. An hour had passed by the time she'd finished her rounds. Everyone had paid.

She stopped at the bank. "Hello, Mr. Jeffers."

"Good morning, Miss Hastings. How may I help you today?"

"I have a deposit." She placed her purse on the counter and reached in for the small bundle of cash and coins she'd just collected. He handed her a slip of paper, and she wrote out her deposit and signed it.

Mr. Jeffers rechecked her math. Finding no error, he signed the receipt. "You have a fine dowry building up, Miss Hastings."

"Thank you, Mr. Jeffers."

"I wish my Susan was more like you. That girl spends money as soon as she earns it. She has to have the newest hat, dress or purse that has come out on the market. Her mother and I are praying she finds a wealthy husband." He chuckled.

Mercy joined in. "She's only sixteen, Mr. Jeffers. Give her a chance."

"I hope you're right. She's not understood the value of a dollar since the day she was born. Perhaps it was Vivian's fault, always dressing her up in the fanciest of dresses. The poor dear has no other desire."

"What if she were to start drawing or creating her own dress designs?" Mercy suggested.

Mr. Jeffers's eyebrows rose toward his balding head. "You know, I've never thought of that. Don't men design most of the ladies' wear?"

"I honestly couldn't tell you. But if your daughter were, as you say, interested in clothing, she'd know what looks good and feels even better than some of the outfits. Just look at those bustles coming out of Paris and London. What woman would be able to sit down in those?"

Mr. Jeffers chuckled again. "I'm mighty glad you came in today, Miss Hastings."

"I look forward to hearing what Susan's thoughts of our discussion are. Have a pleasant day, Mr. Jeffers."

Mercy headed toward the front door and paused when Mr. Jeffers called out, "And you, Miss Hastings. Oh…is it true that Mr. Darling is staying out at your place?"

"Yes, sir." Mercy turned and faced him. "How do you know Mr. Darling?"

"I'm afraid everyone in town knows about Mr. Darling's unfortunate attack, but I am—or rather, I was—his banker."

"Oh, dear. So you're well aware of what was stolen from him." Mercy wanted to know the full sum of money but thought it impolite to ask.

"I'm afraid so. The sheriff verified the amount, but I am not at liberty to say, you understand."

Mercy felt the heat of shame stain her cheeks. "Forgive me. I wasn't asking. Albeit, I am curious. But it is not my place to know such details."

"Please pass on my prayers to Mr. Darling. Let him know his accounts are safe with me."

"Yes, sir." Thoroughly embarrassed, Mercy hustled out of the bank and headed for Pedro's restaurant. She had left home without packing a meal, which meant she would spend money she generally saved. Or she could wait until she returned home.

The tempting aromas from Pedro's won. Mercy found a roadside table and sat down.

"Miss Hastings, it is a pleasure to see you today. What can I serve you?" Maria, Pedro's wife, asked. Her black hair was gathered in the back, and her brown eyes sparkled with joy.

Mercy smiled in response. "I left home without lunch. Can I have a couple burritos to take with me, please?"

"You cannot sit for a while and enjoy your meal?"

"No. I left Mr. Darling at the doctor's office and should return right away." Mercy scanned the street, hoping to get a glimpse of their wagon coming around the corner from the doctor's office.

"*Sí,* I understand. I will tell Pedro to prepare your order right away. Can I get you something to drink?"

"Water with lime, please." Water in St. Augustine had a definite sulfur taste to it. At their farm the water was purer. When drinking the water from the city wells, Mercy always added some citrus. Limes and lemons were her first choices. Orange and grapefruit would work in a pinch.

"*Sí,* I will be right back."

Mercy surveyed the people going about their business on the main street. The city was growing. The old schoolhouse sat on the road close to the old city gates. She shifted her gaze across the way to the timeworn fort. For years, it had guarded the city. During the war, in 'sixty-one, the Union Army abandoned it. Then the Confederacy abandoned it in 'sixty-two. After that, it was used as a prison. Mercy watched the prison guards as they stood overlooking the courtyard below. A shiver of reality overtook her. Could a prisoner have escaped and taken Wyatt Darling's money?

"Here is your *agua,* Miss Hastings. Are you certain I can give you nothing else?"

"Quite. Thank you." Mercy took the wedge of lime and squeezed it into her glass. "Has anyone escaped recently?"

"No, the sheriff, he checked. It was not a prisoner

who attacked Senor Darling. There are not many there right now. Not since the war ended. Still, some men who are in trouble with the military…they stay in the prison."

"Thank you, Maria."

"You are welcome. I will return soon with your burritos."

"¡Gracias!"

"De nada." Maria walked back to the kitchen.

The restaurant was open to the air. The cooking area had a roof, but the sides of the establishment were open, providing shade to the inside during the day and protection at night when they were closed. Most of the tables were outside. They were small, round and big enough for two plates, nothing more. There had been times in the past when Mercy had seen planks spread across several tables to make one long table while a fiesta of music and people filled the small courtyard.

Today, however, there was only one other couple sitting at the far end of the courtyard, smiling and looking for all the world as a couple in love. Mercy cast her gaze away. Would she ever know those feelings?

Wyatt Darling's healing face and his chocolate-brown eyes came to mind. The swelling had gone down on just about all his facial features. He still appeared to have been badly injured, but from what she saw now, he had the possibility of being a rather handsome man.

Maria walked over to her table with a small crock. "Pedro, he says to give you this. He says Mr. Darling, he is not to pay."

"But—"

"No, Miss Hastings, you are not to pay for him. Pedro, he will not take no for an answer. He is a good man, my Pedro."

"*Sí,* a very good man. Tell him I thank him and I know Mr. Darling will, too. I'll return the crock tomorrow."

Maria smiled. "We trust you, Mercy."

Mercy leaned over and gave Maria a kiss on the cheek. Unlike the French, the Spanish only kissed one cheek, whereas the French kissed the air alongside both cheeks.

She headed down the street toward the doctor's office. She quickened her pace when she heard a man's scream coming from inside. She burst through the door to see the ugly open wound on Wyatt's leg. Sweat beaded on her upper lip, her arms, everywhere. The room began to swim. She took a step forward, then collapsed.

Chapter 4

Wyatt's eyes watered from the pain. Dr. Peck, in his infinite wisdom, decided to remove the cast and cleanse the wound. With regard to the itching, he'd been told to get used to it. An uncontrollable scream passed his lips as the good doctor poured something on the wound. Over the years, he'd thought himself a pain-tolerant man. He'd experienced gut-wrenching agony in the past, but this injury brought it to an entirely new level. But he would endure, if it meant he wouldn't lose his leg.

The door flew open. Mercy plunged in. She glanced over and instantly paled. Wyatt started to get up, but the stars he saw prevented him from moving. Dr. Peck caught her head before it hit the floor.

"Is she...?"

"She'll be fine. She just fainted." Dr. Peck carried her to the bed in the backroom. He came back with a thick leather strap. "Here, bite down on this so we don't have any more women barging in and passing out."

"Thanks." Wyatt sank his teeth into the dry leather and clenched even more as the doctor resumed his excruciating work.

"Has the sheriff heard anything?"

Wyatt shook his head. Why was it that doctors and dentists would ask all kinds of questions when you couldn't answer them? Wyatt opened his jaw and let the leather belt tumble down his chest.

"The infection is limited to one bad area. I should cut it out. Brace yourself."

Wyatt groaned. The doctor gave him another sip of the laudanum-laced whiskey to ease the pain. Wyatt placed the leather strap back between his teeth. The doctor took a small pair of scissors from the table beside them.

Wyatt fought with every bit of his strength to stay still and keep from yelling. Tears flowed down his cheeks. The pain burned. He gripped the examining table tighter. He'd seen men have portions of their limbs cut off before. Never had he expected to feel a tiny bit of that pain. He hardened his resolve. He would not cry out again. If Dr. Peck ever had to sever his leg, he'd make sure he had enough whiskey to pass out. *Dear Lord, please heal my leg.* Sparks of light flickered through his closed eyelids as the doctor cut his flesh. His skin felt clammy. His head started to swim. He bit down some more. Then, as quickly as the pain had begun, it ended. He opened his eyes and saw Dr. Peck pulling the scissors back.

"You did well, Wyatt. Let me pack this wound then we can rebuild that cast again."

The plaster cast protected his leg against innocent bangs from others, not to mention a few of his own. He'd never tell Mercy this, but she'd hit it unaware and sent a surge of pain up his leg. Then again, that pain was nothing compared to what he'd just experienced.

"The worst is over." The doctor stood, dropped his metal tools into a basin, then washed his hands, which he dried on a white towel.

Mercy's gentle moans grabbed his attention. Dr. Peck stood up. "I'll be right back. I need to check on my other patient."

Grateful for the reprieve, Wyatt eased out a pent-up breath.

"Wyatt," Dr. Peck called. "I'm getting my sister, Becca, to sit with Miss Hastings."

He nodded. Wyatt scanned the familiar walls that had been his home for more hours than he cared to remember. Dr. Peck returned and continued his healing torture. Wyatt had never been so grateful as to feel the heat from the plaster drying. "You're healing well," Dr. Peck said as he removed the stitches over his right eye. "How's your vision?"

"Fine. It hurts to smile still."

"You'll feel a lot better once the stitches on your cheek are removed. I'm going to leave one in. One area needs to heal further. Come to town in a couple days, and I'll take it out."

"Thank you."

"You're welcome. I'm sure you've seen your fair share of men losing a limb. Truthfully, the infection I was cutting out was just as painful, if not more so, as an amputation."

"Don't remind me. I'd prefer to keep my leg."

"You will. As I said, there was very little infection and you are healing well. You may come in, Miss Hastings."

"Thank you. I'm sorry. I've seen blood before. It's never affected me like that."

"Seeing an open wound is shocking. It's not the same as slaughtering an animal for meal preparations," Dr. Peck offered.

Mercy shook her head no. Wyatt couldn't blame her. It was a nasty-looking wound. "Miss Hastings, Dr. Peck says I'll need to stay here for another hour. I'd be happy to stay the night in town rather than have you wait on me."

Mercy turned her head and stared at him. "I don't mind waiting. Or I can pick you up tomorrow after my deliveries."

"That would be fine. Doctor, is it all right if I spend the night on your cot?"

"Ah, sure. I'll let my sisters know so they can prepare for an overnight dinner guest."

"Don't bother. I'm fairly certain I can make it to Pedro's for dinner."

"Speaking of Pedro…" Mercy walked back into the room where she had recovered. "He gave me these for our lunch. You can have them both. I'll pick up something from home." She handed him the crock and left.

Wyatt stared at the door. Time apart would be good for both of them. His feelings for Mercy were developing in a way he should never allow. She was ten years his junior, and he had nothing to offer a woman. He'd decided many years ago not to take a wife.

"Mind telling me what that was all about?" Dr. Peck asked.

"I didn't want to impose upon the Hastings family. They are generous people, but I feel I need to spend more time in town and try to figure out what I'm going to do with myself."

"You're going to take the time to recover, or you'll lose your leg. Understand me when I say this, if you start pushing yourself and forcing your body to do more than it is capable of right now, you could very well lose that limb or worse. The body needs recovery time. Unfortunately, you, Mr. Darling, are not a patient man. You're wanting everything yesterday, with no regard to your health."

Wyatt felt duly chastised. "Yes, sir. I'll heed your warnings."

"Good. Now rest while I ask Mary to make up a cot for you. You're right, the Hastings are fine folks. Respect them enough to tell them the truth about your feelings of insecurity."

Wyatt cleared his throat. He never thought of himself as insecure before. He'd learned his trade and learned it well. His captains depended upon him. The men under him showed the right amount of respect. So why couldn't he relax?

"Because you're not an idle man," he said to the empty room. He would miss Mrs. Hastings's cooking and the rest of the family tonight. He liked all of them. His growing attraction to Mercy was a stumbling block. But where else could he live with no means to support himself? He couldn't, and that was the problem. Despite all the generous offers of help from the citizens of St. Augustine, no other family had come forward to put him up.

The doctor said it would take a month or more before he could walk, and even then, he'd still be using crutches. He couldn't get a job on board a ship until he was free of the props.

Mary Peck stepped into the room. "Mr. Darling, I understand you'll be spending a night with us tonight." She seemed friendly enough—no, that wasn't it—professional. She assisted her brother in the office but was not friendly to the point of wanting to get to know the patients.

"Yes, miss. Thank you."

"Can I fetch you anything to make your stay more comfortable?" She seemed to smile as an afterthought, confirming his prior opinion.

"No, thank you." He looked down at his leg. "Wait. Yes, if you could please. I would like a paper and pen. I'd like to compose a letter."

"I'll bring them down after I make up your bed. The doctor said you need to stay put for a while."

"Yes, I'm aware."

She nodded and went back into the room.

He did have some assets, and it was high time he made use of them. He penned a letter to Jason Smith, his caretaker in Cotuit Port. He'd have some funds sent down here, and after they arrived, he'd return home to Cape Cod. He could oversee his property while he waited for his leg to heal and then put some distance between him and Mercy Hastings.

In the meantime, knowing he would be leaving soon gave him a sense of peace about staying with the Hastings family. He could deal with temptation for a couple of weeks. Images of Mercy flashed through his mind. *Lord, give me strength.*

Mercy didn't know how to explain what had happened at the doctor's office. She'd seen blood before. She'd even seen deep wounds. But something about the cries of pain and seeing Wyatt's open flesh took a toll.

"Where is Mr. Darling?" Ben grasped the bridle of the horse and led him toward the stable.

Mercy placed the reins down on the footboard. "He's

staying overnight at Dr. Peck's. The doctor changed the plaster cast and cleaned his wound."

"I wish I'd been there," Ben said with an eagerness that made Mercy's stomach flip. "Dad's in the house. He's been mumbling all afternoon. I think he's worried you and Mr. Darling are becoming too close."

Mercy knew a gentle pink was developing on her cheeks. She turned her head and checked the wagon for her purse. "There's nothing going on."

"Still, he's concerned about proper behavior. He suggests that I accompany you and Mr. Darling next time."

"I don't have a problem with that. If you weren't in school, I would have encouraged you to go in with Mr. Darling. I have some orders I need to get to work on."

Ben smiled. "Great. I like him. He's quiet and keeps to himself. But there's something about him. I can't place my finger on it. But I think it has to do with him working so hard for his dream. You know?"

She did know. Wyatt Darling was a hardworking man who'd suffered a lot in his thirty years. "I think I do."

"I'll take care of JoJo while you get started on your washing."

"Thanks, Ben."

"You're welcome, sis." Ben led JoJo into the barn. Mercy headed over to her work area and lit a fire, then went to the well and pumped out what she needed to wash the white towels for Mr. Billings's Tropical Breezes Inn. Thankfully, the days were getting longer and she'd be able to have all the sheets dry before nightfall. Which gave her plenty of time to consider what had transpired between her and Wyatt. He'd seemed genuinely cold and distant after she fainted. Had she embarrassed him?

The question plagued Mercy for most of the afternoon and into the evening. She obviously cared too much. If it wasn't for her job, she'd be tempted to take a trip and visit some of her relatives. On the other hand, would Mr. Darling find another location to spend his recovery days? If so, she had nothing to be concerned about. Then again, did she have genuine affection for Wyatt, or were these merely fantasies of her own desire to find someone she could spend the rest of her life with?

She was of age, even past it by some people's accounts. Her parents had encouraged her to wait for a suitor until she was in her late teens. When she was sixteen, she thought them horribly unfair. Then, as time progressed, she saw the wisdom of her parents' counsel. So many of her thoughts and perspectives had changed since she was sixteen. Perhaps too many. One day, she'd heard some men discussing future wives, and her name had come up. Her ability to run her own business was a threat to most of the men in the circle. Several worried that she'd even compromised her virtue. Mercy knew that wasn't true, but she discovered something else about herself that day. She discovered a strength in her own personal knowledge of who she was in God's eyes, and He alone knew all her shortcomings and failures. Meaningless social encounters and the driving need to find a husband no longer held an appeal. Instead, she worked harder to build up her business.

With Wyatt Darling staying in her barn, she had lost sight of that goal. She had begun to think about marriage, building a life together, children and a future. It seemed foolish now, looking back on the past week. What did she even know about him? They easily engaged in conversation but had never touched on anything of substance. Mercy closed her eyes and fell to her knees. *Father, forgive me. I let my wishes run ahead of anyone You might have in mind for me to marry. If Wyatt is the man, then make it clear to both of us. If he is not, remove these foolish dreams from me.*

"Mercy?" Her mother rushed to her side. "Are you all right?"

Mercy wiped her eyes. "I'm fine, Mother. I was simply praying."

"Forgive my intrusion. Is there anything I can do? I have a good ear."

"No, I don't believe anyone can help me with these emotions."

"Ah, so you've been praying about Mr. Darling."

Mercy stood up and brushed off her skirt. She turned from her mother and nodded her head in agreement.

Rosemarie Hastings sat down on a small wooden barrel. "He's a fine man but there are too many secrets buried in his soul, I fear. Your father's been concerned about your growing interest in Mr. Darling."

"I gathered that from something Ben said earlier. Nothing has transpired between us, Mother. He's been a perfect gentleman." She turned and faced her mother. "These are my own foolish yearnings. I was so content with my life before Mr. Darling came across my path. My business is going well. I no longer felt the need to have a man in my life. I'd love to marry and have children one day, but that driving desire that I had when I was sixteen passed a long time ago. I've found contentment in my life."

"Mercy, how did it make you feel when Jack and Diane had their baby?"

Mercy looked into the deep pool of blue in her mother's eyes and smiled. "I was very happy for them. But, yes, I hungered to have my own child."

"I know. Honey, I can't say that you will be married one day. I believe it to be true and I've prayed for your husband from time to time. Wyatt Darling is ten years your senior. Perhaps that isn't too much of a spread, but then again, there is a lot of growing that happens to a person from the age of twenty to the age of thirty.

"Ben said Mr. Darling would be spending the night with the doctor. If he should return, he's welcome to. However, if he does, I'm going to have Amy and Bessie take him his meals. You've fallen behind in your work since he arrived."

Mercy hadn't missed a step with a customer, but her household chores were lacking. "I'm sorry."

Rosemarie got up from her stool. "Never mind about that. I, actually your father and I, both feel you need to put some distance between the two of you. We're not saying don't spend any time with him, but restrict it. Keep your priorities in mind."

"Yes, ma'am." The image of Wyatt driving the wagon came back to mind. "I think Mr. Darling is capable of going to town on his own from now on."

Her mother smiled. "Yes, I believe you are right. When you're done with your laundry, I could use a batch of soap."

"I'll make the lye tonight."

Rosemarie tapped her on the shoulder. "Thank you, dear. I'll see you in the house for supper."

Mercy went back to work. Her mother's words replayed in her mind several times. What was her intention? Last week, it was to be a Good Samaritan. Was that all she was supposed to be for Wyatt Darling, his Good Samaritan? The biblical story played over in her mind once again. After the Good Samaritan provided for the wounded man, he left and moved on with his life. Was that what she'd been doing wrong? Had she been trying to hold on to helping Wyatt?

Her focus had been wrong. She'd focused on the man, then she'd focused on her own desires. Mercy closed her eyes and prayed again. *Father, forgive me.*

The weight that had been on her shoulders since the doctor's office lifted. Mercy went back to work and after her laundry was finished, she gathered the ashes and put them in the bin. Creating lye was dirty work. White sheets and towels needed to be out of the way before one could start on the project. In a few days, she would gather up the fat from the recently butchered steer. Father had the animal hanging in the salt house, aging. The salt was a natural source to keep the humidity down and the bacteria from rotting the meat.

Beef that had been aged was more tender and flavorful, in her opinion. Of course, the fact that she'd grown up in the house where her father had invested so much in the process might have something to do with her own preferences.

Soon it would be time to harvest more salt from the sea. One could do it at any season but the summer months were best. With the hot temperatures, the evaporation process was quicker. Gathering salt was an event that allowed the family to have a vacation of a sort. The family would camp out at the shore for a few nights. They set up a kettle on the beach and boiled the water down and scraped out the salt, repeating the process over and over again until they had enough barrels filled to supply the family's needs for a year.

She wouldn't be able to keep up with her customers while harvesting the salt this year. She'd have to ask her good friend, Grace Martin, to give her a hand. She and Grace were old schoolmates. Grace had married young and was widowed less than a year later. Grace's parents were not as progressive as Mercy's. She could work, but even though she was a widow, she had been required to move back to her parents' home. At first, Grace didn't mind. But as time had gone by, she hungered for the opportunity to live on her own and provide for herself. Unfortunately, Mercy's laundry business wasn't large enough to support another employee. But when she could, Mercy would hire Grace to work here and there for her, and harvesting the salt was a good opportunity to hire Grace.

Mercy's hand slipped. "Ouch." She nicked her finger. She quickly cleansed the wound and wrapped it with a small cotton strip. She thought of harvesting the salt with a slight cut and how the salt would sting. The gash in Wyatt's leg came back to mind. Mercy felt faint. She grabbed the wooden tabletop and steadied herself. Salt in that wound would have made him scream even louder. "Father, heal him quickly," she prayed and finished filling the trough with ash to make the lye.

After the dirty process of shoveling was over, Mercy felt the need for a shower. Instead, she decided on a quick swim in the Matanzas River. Its brackish waters were cleansing enough to remove the ash from her body and yet not salty enough to leave her skin feeling itchy. Swimming wasn't something people did on a regular basis, but there was a cove on the river behind her house where it was private enough not to offend those who felt it unbecoming for a lady to splash around. Admittedly, Mercy liked the feel of the water and enjoyed the exercise, although she hadn't had much time for it lately. Of course, it was still spring and the water was a bit chilly.

The rest of the day and evening went without a hitch,

and Mercy realized she was thinking less and less about Wyatt Darling.

The next day Wyatt returned with Ben. Over the next couple of days, Mercy kept pace with her customers and their needs.

She was on her way home with a full wheelbarrow when Robbie Brown called out. "Mercy, Wait a minute."

She put down her load and waited for him. Robbie had gone to school with Mercy years ago. He'd stopped attending when he started working for his family lumber business. "Hi, what do you need?" she asked, cupping her hand over her eyes to watch him jog toward her. Robbie had broad shoulders and well-rounded muscles from working at his father's business.

"Not much. I saw you walking with this heavy burden and thought I could lend you a hand. How have you been? I haven't seen you in a long time."

Robbie had been one of the men in the gathering who had spoken harshly about her and her business. "I'm fine." *What is he after?*

"Mercy…" He grabbed the wooden handles of her wheelbarrow. "I've been thinkin' about settling down lately, and I was wondering if you might be interested in discussing a potential future."

Mercy stopped dead in her tracks. Was this some cruel joke? Robbie was pleasant enough on the eyes, and he seemed to have a good head on his shoulders, but he wasn't a reader and he… "I don't understand. Why me?"

"I've always had an eye for you, since you were thirteen. You were one of the prettiest gals in school and, well, I thought perhaps it was time to settle down and have some children." He continued pushing the cart forward.

Mercy followed. "Robbie, I think I'm flattered, but

I'm more curious. Weren't you one of the men who was discussing me a couple years ago, saying all sorts of horrible things about how I wouldn't make a good wife? How I didn't know my place…" She let her words trail off.

"You heard all that?" His face flamed. "I'm sorry. I can't speak for the rest of the men, but we were foolish. I mean, you're smart and energetic. You'd do well raising a pack of children. I'm hoping to have at least eight." Robbie smiled.

Mercy didn't know if she wanted eight children. She certainly didn't have any romantic interest in Robbie. "What about love, romance?"

"That's the stuff of stupid novels. I'm talking about a real wife. One who knows how to tend to a house, raise children and fix good meals. You excel in all those areas." He beamed.

There was no question he'd given this some serious thought, and while it would be nice to marry, she still held on to her ideas of romance. "Thank you for your kind offer, but my answer is no."

"You're kidding, right? I don't know of anyone else offering. You want to get married, don't ya?"

"Perhaps. I'm content with my life as it is right now. Mother and Father enjoy my help around the house, my business is going well, and I look forward to quiet evenings, reading books and not fretting about the house and what needs to be done for the morning breakfast."

"You are a peculiar person, Mercy Hastings. If you don't mind, I'll ask your father for your hand."

Mercy stopped and planted her hands on her hips. "You will not."

"Mercy, be reasonable. I'm a good man. I don't look

that bad and I have a piece of land to build my own house on. What's not to like?"

Your attitude? "Robbie, my answer is no. Even if you were to convince my father, my answer would still be no."

"We'll see." Robbie continued walking her laundry back to her home.

Mercy stomped behind him. *How dare he think he can just order me to be his wife?* And for what reason, to give him a comfortable home and bear his babies? *What kind of life is that?* She prayed her father would see through such a horrible proposal and not subject her to any kind of courtship with the man.

Life sure was simpler before Wyatt Darling came to town.

Wyatt hobbled around his room and straightened his bed. He still couldn't get up on a horse, but he could drive a wagon. With nothing compelling him to go to town, he ached to do something. There were no leads on the robbers. Mr. Jeffers at the bank had verified the amount of money he'd withdrawn. The reality that his money was gone came home like the morning tide, full and lapping at his dreams. And just as quickly, his dreams rode out with the tide, leaving him feeling very much alone and without purpose.

Jackson Hastings came into the barn. Wyatt readied his crutches to have some conversation with someone, anyone. He'd hardly seen Mercy since he'd given her such a rude send-off. He'd started to leave his room when he heard, "Mr. Hastings, I'd like to have a word with you, sir."

"Ignore him, Father. I have." The lilt of Mercy's voice caused him to smile.

The stranger chuckled. "That's only because she hasn't gotten to know me yet. Mr. Hastings, I'd like to ask your permission to court Mercy."

Mercy let out an exasperated sigh and stomped off to the house. Wyatt stayed put, not wanting to step into this storm. He wondered how Jackson Hastings would approach this problem.

"And who might you be, boy?"

"Sorry, sir. My name is Robert Brown. My father is Lloyd Brown. We live in the Sebastian area. My father has a lumber business. Most folks call me Robbie."

"I know who your father is, son. Why would you approach me when it is clear that Mercy is not interested in a possible courtship with you?"

"You know women, sir. They don't know what they want until you tell 'em. I know that given half a chance, Mercy will agree I would make a fine husband and father to our children."

Jackson laughed. "I see. And you've said all this to my daughter?"

"Yes, sir."

"When, pray tell?"

"A few minutes ago, on our way here."

Wyatt held back his own laughter. The boy had the wits of a gnat. Then again, he seemed to know what he wanted, unlike him. Still, he couldn't see Mercy married to a man like that.

"I see, so before you even spoke of your love and affection, you presumed upon my daughter and myself your intentions to marry her."

"Yes, sir." Robbie's voice faltered.

"Tell me, Robbie, what does the Bible say about love?"

"That God is love, and we are to love as He has loved

us." Robbie cleared his throat. "Mr. Hastings, I know Mercy doesn't love me and I don't love her, but given time, perhaps that will change. I believe a woman such as your daughter would make a fine wife. She's pleasant on the eyes, she knows how to care for a house, can cook, clean, sew and I've seen her with her younger sisters. I know she'll be good with my children. She's a good choice, Sir."

"Yes, she is. On that point, I will agree with you. However, you do not have my blessing. You do, however, have the right to try and woo and change her mind. If she decides she is interested in courting you, then I will reconsider. However, you'd do well to learn a bit more about women, son. They do not like to be ordered about. They are smart and true helpmates if you allow them to be. Some of the stupidest men I've seen are ones who don't listen to their wives."

"Thank you, sir. I'm sure I can convince her." Robbie ran out of the barn.

Jackson Hastings slapped the post with a leather whip. "God protect her!" he moaned.

Wyatt stepped from his room into the barn and cleared his throat. "I couldn't help but overhear."

"That boy is so confident in himself, he didn't hear a single word I said." Jackson sighed.

"Has Mercy had many suitors?"

"No. A couple years back some men got to discussing Mercy and thought her not worth the risk. I hated for Mercy to hear those hurtful things, but it was a blessing. For two years, I didn't have the likes of Robbie Brown running around my ranch. I fear he will be the first in a long line of suitors, none of them qualified or worthy of my daughter's affections."

Wyatt took in a deep pull of air and leaned harder

on his crutches. "I'll add to your prayers for Mercy's protection."

"Thank you. She's a rare gem and I would hate to see her hurt."

A knot twisted in Wyatt's gut. He'd hurt Mercy. Was Jackson Hastings aware? "How did you know what these young men said about Mercy?"

"Mercy overheard them. She cried herself to sleep that night. But there was a change in her after that. She was more confident in who God designed her to be. As I said, it was a blessing. God took something horrible and made her stronger from it. However, sir, you are a visitor in our home and this is a private matter, so I shall not discuss it further."

"I understand. If I am a burden, I can secure a room at the inn. I have some funds being sent to me shortly. I own some property up north, and my caretaker has been renting it out for me for the past thirteen years. I've never drawn from the account, so there should be a fair amount in savings."

Jackson shook his head no. "You're welcome to stay here, son. What did Dr. Peck say about your leg?"

"That it is healing well. I still cannot step on it for five more weeks. And even then, it will only be with crutches and a lighter cast, probably for two months. My goal is to go north and oversee my property while I recover. After that, I'll reevaluate my future. In the meantime I will have to wait for the post to arrive."

"Can you ride a horse?"

"If I can figure out how to get on and off without putting any weight on my right leg. As you know, you mount a horse on the left side."

"True, but let me think." Jackson scanned the barn. "Ah, I've got it. Follow me." Jackson led the horse toward the house and up to the porch. "Step up onto the porch and come over to this side, then slide down on to the saddle."

Wyatt did as told. He trembled at first, on his way down, but once there, he felt the confidence of the animal.

"Good, good. Ride with me. I need to check my stock."

With a gentle nudge, he encouraged the animal forward and followed Jackson back to the barn. A surge of joy swept through him as Wyatt felt the freedom the horse gave him to move about. He paused at the entrance. The young man who had been in the barn not long ago now faced Mercy a short distance away, aggressively trying to convince her to court him. She backed away, and he grabbed Mercy's arm and squeezed. Wyatt kicked the horse into gear. "Unhand her," Wyatt boomed.

Jackson fired his shotgun. The boy paled. Mercy stared.

Chapter 5

Mercy stepped back. Father cocked his shotgun, ready if needed. Wyatt nudged JoJo closer to Mercy, his brand new cast gleaming white. Robbie stood there, frozen with fear.

"Son, I believe you have your answer. You can go now," her father declared.

"Yes, sir. Sorry, sir." Robbie turned back to Mercy. Her heart sank. The poor boy didn't have a clue as to what she would look for in a husband. He thought all he had to do was provide for a wife and live his own life. Where was the joy in a relationship like that? She was still puzzled by Robbie's proclamation that he wanted to marry her. It didn't make sense.

"Are you all right, Mercy?" Father whispered.

"I'm fine. He just wouldn't accept no for an answer." Mercy turned toward her father. "He said he had your permission to try and convince me."

"That he did, daughter. I figured you'd give him a piece of your mind, and he'd run off scareder than a rabbit trapped in a field with a hawk hungry for breakfast."

Wyatt sat silently on his horse. Mercy turned toward him. "You're able to ride now?"

"Your father figured a way for me to get on. Yes. It feels good."

"Well, enjoy your ride. I need to get back to work." Mercy returned to her wash and turned her back on the two men. Robbie had frightened her. He kept pushing. He wouldn't stop trying to convince her. It was odd, really. She'd never experienced anything like that before. He seemed desperate, unlike his casual approach on the road before they arrived at the house. Why was he so convinced she'd make him a good wife? And did that really matter? He didn't want a wife. He wanted a breeder and a housekeeper. She wanted to go back to bed and restart the day. The frantic look in Robbie's eyes plagued her. She'd never seen that look before.

Mercy rubbed her arms. Perhaps she should hire Grace now and take a few days off, working on the salt harvesting. But the thought of being alone on the beach overnight in a tent did not appeal to her at all. Staying home in the protection of her family seemed a wiser decision. She grabbed the bucket of ash and dumped it in the trough.

Suspended by four poles, the trough stood over a small table with a basin to collect the lye that leaked through. She covered the ash with water and let it sit. Tomorrow she would repeat the process again. Three days were needed to make the lye, but in the end they would have a large enough batch to make soap. Leftover lye would be saved for later use.

She kept herself busy with work through dinner. She

read, then retired for the evening. No one mentioned the incident with Robbie, and Mercy was grateful. Every time she thought of him pushing her to see his way of thinking about marriage and remembered that desperation in his eyes… It left her unsettled.

The next few days passed with no further incidents, allowing Mercy to feel comfortable walking alone into town. Ever since the other day when Robbie had come up to her, she'd been looking over her shoulder, worried he'd pop out from behind a sable palm. Thankfully, that fear was not answered. Today was a new day. The sun was shining. The gulls were hunting their breakfast in the harbor. Life in St. Augustine was getting back to normal. Even thoughts of Wyatt Darling were limited to prayers for his healing. Well, most of the time. There were some fanciful dreams of marrying him. She pictured him in his navy blue captain's uniform at the front of the church. Standing, not on crutches but upright and regal. Mercy smiled at the image.

A gull cawed and brought her back to reality. Fantasy was just that, fantasy. Wyatt Darling loved the sea and wasn't all that interested in much else. Although he was beginning to talk at the dinner table about his home in Cotuit Port, Massachusetts, and of his returning there once he was able to put some weight on his leg. Which, according to Dr. Peck, would be in a month.

Wyatt's face was healing well. The jagged red scars were turning pink. He was a handsome man.

"Mercy!" Grace Martin waved from across the street.

Mercy pushed her wheelbarrow over the walkway. "Hi, Grace, how are you? It's so good to see you. I've been meaning to stop by and ask you if you would be up for a few days of work next week."

"You're the answer to my prayers. If I have to stay

cooped in with my parents for another day with no direction for the future, I'll jump the next ship out of here."

Mercy chuckled. "I wish I had enough work to hire you."

"That's why I was looking for you. I think, with a little effort on my part, we could have enough clients to pay me a small salary. I was also wondering if you thought your parents might rent out that room in the barn that they're letting that stranger use."

"First, his name is Wyatt Darling, and he won't be leaving for another month. Second, I need to deliver these items before I lose a customer I have now. Follow me. We can talk along the way."

Grace picked up her skirt ever so slightly and walked alongside Mercy. Mercy had hemmed up her work dresses an inch or two higher than was customary to prevent tripping over them while pushing her wheelbarrow or carrying an armful of laundry.

"So, tell me, what's the problem with your parents now?"

"They're talking suitors. They want me to get married again. I don't know if I can risk losing someone else. Micah and I weren't married long but I still love him and miss him terribly."

"You'll find someone when the time is right."

Grace smiled. "How is it your parents aren't pushing you?"

"I'm blessed." Actually, her parents were trying to keep her and Wyatt apart. Mercy frowned. Did her parents not want her to marry? The conversation she had with her mother the other day came back to mind. No, they were praying for her spouse and trusting the Lord for His provision.

"Don't remind me. I know I shouldn't be upset with my parents. They just want what is best for me. To tell you the truth, there are moments when I hunger to have someone I can snuggle and share my thoughts with. Micah and I, we had some grand dreams. Probably foolish ones, but they were our dreams and now…" Grace's words trailed off.

Mercy put down the wheelbarrow and scooped Grace up in a hug. "I'm sorry for your loss. I can't imagine how hard it is to lose someone."

Grace sniffed, then pulled out of the embrace. "Sorry, I don't mean to be so melancholy." She dabbed her eyes and cheeks free of her tears. "I really do have an idea for how we can increase your business enough so that I can work for you."

Mercy lifted the handles of the wheelbarrow and pushed forward. "Do tell."

Grace went on to explain how they could pick up a few more customers and how two could get the work done quicker than one. Truthfully, Mercy had wanted to find more work, but she had reached the capacity of what she could get done in a day. She'd even given thought to using the wagon every morning. It saved time on the delivery and pickup. Walking back and forth to town took an hour each way. A wagon could do it in fifteen to twenty minutes.

"Let's pray about it, Grace. I'd like to help you out, but I'd have to buy another pot for boiling the laundry, another washboard and other tools so that we could both work at the same time."

"Hmm, I hadn't thought about the pot. I've got a washboard. It was a wedding present."

"I was going to ask you to work for me next week so I could do some salt harvesting. Are you interested?"

"Does a gull like fish? Of course. Which days?"

"I haven't decided. In fact, I haven't spoken with my parents about it. I noticed the salt was getting low when I checked on the fat for soap making." Mercy paused. "Mr. Billings mentioned his frustration with one of the girls who did housekeeping for the rooms. You might check with him about a job. I don't know what the pay is, and I don't know if your father would approve, but I've heard some of the women get mighty fine tips every once in a while. Then there are times when they don't receive a penny. It's not a very rewarding job."

"Frankly, I'd do anything to be rid of my parents trying to control my life. I am an adult and I have been married. Perhaps, they would have treated me differently if we'd had a child. There are days I wish we had not decided to wait. I'd still have a piece of Micah with me. Then again, it might make the ache even harder."

Compassion for Grace grew. Mercy really didn't understand the depth of loneliness and frustration that her friend endured from day to day. She fired off a simple prayer for God's peace and sustaining grace in her friend's life. "Let's work together today and go over your thoughts for building up my business."

A smile erupted from ear to ear on Grace's face. "Thank you."

Mercy's mind swirled with possible scenarios of how to employ Grace. She could work less and allow Grace the additional income. Mercy didn't have the driving need to be out on her own. Of course, she'd never known that independence, so she didn't know what she might be missing. All she knew was ranch life, which started at the crack of dawn and ended right after you laid your head on the pillow. Everyone worked. Mercy couldn't imagine living alone and having to do all the chores. Of course, she wouldn't have to cook for anyone but herself, and cleanup would be much less. Perhaps Grace was on to something.

"I'm sorry, Mr. Darling. There hasn't been any sign of your stolen money. It's as if it never existed. No one has spent more than his or her usual amounts. And unfortunately you didn't manage to hurt your attackers enough to have left a visible trace," Sheriff Bower said as he sat down behind his desk. The room was small and the back half had a holding cell. Fort Marion could house additional prisoners if necessary. The old fort had been built by the Spanish long before the pilgrims came to Plymouth. Which seemed a bit odd, remembering his American history classes. Then again, Florida hadn't become a part of the United States until 'forty-five.

Wyatt thought back on his attack. He balled his fist and released it slowly. "I'm certain I must have landed a blow. I just can't remember. All I can see in my mind's eye is three, dark-hooded men. They were completely covered in black. The next thing I remember is pain and then the pain of waking up."

"I won't stop investigating. If someone from St. Augustine did rob you, they'll come to the surface eventually. As you know, I fear that it might have been someone from a ship. We spoke before on this matter but you were still under the influence of the pain medications the Doc gave you. Did anyone on your crew know your plans?"

A lead weight dropped in the pit of his stomach. "Yes, I'm afraid so. They all knew I was leaving the ship to buy my own. But they wouldn't have known about bringing the cash to James Earl. What did he have to say about that?"

"As I mentioned before, Mr. Earl is very sorry for your loss. He explained his wanting cash because he and his family were moving out to Texas. And your inability to purchase the ship has set him and his family back, as well. They won't be able to leave until the ship is sold."

"I'd love to oblige the man, but I can't." Wyatt scanned the iron bars behind Sheriff Bower, imagining the three men standing behind them.

"I wish I had better news for you, Mr. Darling but…"

"I understand, Sheriff. I'll be returning north in four weeks. If you should recover my money, I'll open an account with the bank again and you can put it in there."

"Leave me your forwarding address and I'll make certain you receive word."

"Thank you." The weight of the world crashed onto his shoulders. He couldn't imagine any more disappointing news. Wyatt didn't realize how much he had hoped Sheriff Bower would have found the men and the money. He pivoted on his crutches and headed out the door. "Good day, Sheriff."

Out in the street, Benjamin Hastings leaned against the wagon. The kid proved to be quite helpful. Jackson Hastings had done a fine job raising his children. They all worked hard and seemed to have an ambition that would bode well in life. Wyatt thought back on his own father, the times together, the instructions given. If he had lived, he imagined his father would be much the same as Jackson Hastings, encouraging and yet demanding independence. He shook away the thoughts and focused back on the wagon. "What do you have there?"

Benjamin beamed. "I found it on the beach."

In the back of the wagon lay some broken remains of a ship. "What on earth do you plan to do with those?"

"Burn them. The salt gives the flames a vibrant color. Copper does, too, but that's expensive. The wood probably won't be dried out in time for the salt harvesting Mercy and I are planning on doing next week, but I'll use it for something. You can't let a good bit of wood go to waste."

"No, I suppose you can't." Wyatt hobbled over to the wagon. His dexterity with the crutches increased each day.

"Wanna stop by Dr. Peck's?"

Not particularly. "I saw him leaving the office when we came into town. Tomorrow I have to come in to have the cast removed and the wound checked again." Wyatt dreaded the cleansing of the wound. He prayed that complete healing had happened and no further treatment was necessary. He didn't want to go through that again.

"Fine, where to?"

"Back to the house, unless you have further errands."

Ben climbed up into the wagon. "Nope. I need to get some sleep. Tonight I'm going shrimping. They're running and I've had a hankering for shrimp."

"I'd love to lend a hand, but I don't think I could do much."

"Not with that leg. We're in the water when we cast the net and pull it to shore. When the shrimp are running like this, you can cast a net off the docks, but I don't think that's wise for you at this time. It would be too easy to get off balance and fall in."

Wyatt chuckled. "You're probably right."

"Tell ya what. You can help me clean 'em. Ma sure would appreciate that."

"I'll be glad to help." Wyatt had enough experience with various types of fish, so he knew chopping off the heads was not the entire process with the crustacean. In fact, the real problem came in the deveining process. It took a while to learn the knack, but he had. And it felt good to finally be contributing to the needs of the family in some way. "On board ship, the men can down many pounds of shrimp. How do you plan on storing them?"

"Mother makes a shrimp sauce that adds flavor to some of the fish dishes she makes. Most will be canned for later use. But there is nothing like fresh shrimp."

"I enjoy them, as well. In Australia, they call them prawns. They are huge shrimp."

"You've been to Australia?"

"One year, when I was eighteen. I thought life would be more exciting going to other countries. And it was, but it came at a high cost."

"How so?"

"Our ship was captured by pirates. Thankfully, the Good Lord spared us, and we were rescued. I decided, as exotic as those countries were, I preferred the safety of American waters. During the war, we met opposition. But at least we were treated with dignity."

"I can't imagine. The history of St. Augustine is not without our own pirates. But you don't know what old tales are true and what are simply just tales. Sailors love to carry on."

Wyatt chuckled again. "That they do."

Ben led the horse-drawn wagon toward the turn-off to their property. Robert Brown jumped out from behind a sable palm. "Ben," he called out.

Wyatt tensed. He didn't have a shotgun handy. Ben pulled the horse to a stop. "What do you want, Robbie."

"To apologize to Mercy. Is she home?"

"I don't think so. If Father catches you lurking in the bushes, he'll shoot ya. You'd best run off."

"Please, tell Mercy I'm sorry. I didn't mean nothin'. Ma says I don't know nothin' about courtin' a girl." Robbie glanced down at his feet and kicked the sand.

Ben and Wyatt snickered.

"Who are you to laugh, mister? Ain't none of your business."

Wyatt didn't trust him. "I suppose it isn't. I heard what you said to Mr. Hastings when you asked to court Mercy. Seems to me you'd best speak with your Momma about how a woman wants to be treated."

"Says you!" Robbie spat on the ground.

Wyatt decided not to say another word. He didn't like the anger he saw in the young man's eyes. Ben, on the other hand, stood up in the wagon. "Robbie, iffin' you know what's best for you, you'll leave and not say another word to my sister. I personally don't think you know how to treat a woman, and I won't have my sister or any other woman I'm close to being a part of your life. You need to change, and listening to your mother is about the best thing you can do. A real man doesn't order a woman around. He invites her to speak her mind."

"Your family is nuts, ya know that? Whoever heard of letting a woman work outside the home? And your father allows your sister to walk alone, back and forth to town. No woman of mine would ever be put into such a compromising position. Not with all the wayward sailors who come to port. And you, sir—" he turned to Wyatt "—know that to be a fact."

Ben jumped down from the wagon. He stood the same height as Robbie but had a smaller build. Wyatt couldn't do much if a fistfight was to break out between the two young men, but he could do something. Wyatt jumped awkwardly down from the wagon.

"Robbie Brown, I'm not a fighting man, but I won't take you speaking poorly of my father or my sister, you hear me?"

Robbie stepped back.

Wyatt came up alongside them. Robbie eyed him. "Fine, I won't say another word. Tell your sister I'm sorry, and I won't be coming to court her no more."

"I think that's best." Benjamin relaxed his rigid stance.

Wyatt and Ben stood there watching Robbie walk back toward town. Ben leaned toward Wyatt. "I'm concerned about Mercy walking back and forth alone."

"Agreed. I don't trust him."

Ben nodded his agreement. "I think he's harmless, but he's always gotten what he wanted when he wanted it. I don't think he really cares for Mercy, or he wouldn't have given up so easily."

Wyatt had to agree. Mercy deserved a man who would love and cherish her. Not some man full of himself and not concerned for anyone else. "She's probably ready to come home. Should we go pick her up?"

Ben nodded. "I think you're right. Let me unload this wood and we'll go back and get her."

Wyatt wondered if he should attempt walking back to the house. If he was careful, he could probably make it. "Ben, I'll walk to the house from here and tell your folks what happened and why you're going to be late."

"Are you sure? I could take you to the house."

"No, I'm sure. You go on ahead."

"Thank you, Wyatt."

They said goodbye and Wyatt hobbled down the dirt road. In places it was hard from the coquina. In other spots, the sand was soft and he could easily misplace his crutches. Which would mean he'd take a tumble, and tumbling down was not in his plans today. Sweat poured down his back. The short walk took excruciating time and energy. At his current rate, he expected to see Ben riding up with Mercy.

As he approached the house, Rosemarie Hastings came running out to greet him. "What's happened? Is Ben all right?"

Chapter 6

After supper Wyatt found himself alone in his room. The family had important matters to discuss, and he wasn't family. Since the death of his, this family had become the closest he had experienced. Captain Nickerson had been good to him, helpful and even treated him like a nephew. He'd protected Wyatt during his younger years, keeping him away from the influences of some of the men. Drinking and carrying on was something that went hand in hand with many sailors, but Captain Nickerson's ships were more tightly run. He didn't allow spirits on board. He didn't deny that the men sneaked them aboard. They knew they'd be set ashore at the next port if they were found drunk and disorderly.

With that background, he'd grown up in a pretty controlled environment, until he went to the South Seas. He'd been keelhauled after the pirates attacked their ship. They killed Captain Holmes and the first mate, hoping they'd find gold. There wasn't any, but the crew were unable to convince them. It took keelhauling Wyatt to persuade them. His back was shredded, and he barely survived the attack. Thankfully, he'd been able to hold his breath long enough, and they were more interested in having him talk, rather than killed. They set him ashore with the rest of the crew who wouldn't change sides.

They spent six months on that island before help arrived. They'd been fortunate, and Wyatt knew God's protection had been on him. He closed his eyes and prayed again for the families of the men who'd been lost. A knock interrupted his prayers. "Come in."

"Mr. Darling." Jackson Hastings came into the room.

Jackson, who generally stood tall and straight, approached with his shoulders slumped. "Mr. Hastings, is something wrong?"

"I'm in need of your assistance."

"Anything I can do, I'm happy to."

"I'm concerned for Mercy and her safety."

Wyatt nodded. He, too, had the same concerns. "However, I'm also concerned about how folks will talk if you are seen alone together over and over again."

Wyatt knitted his eyebrows but didn't speak.

"Forgive me. Let me explain."

"Have a seat," Wyatt offered, then hobbled over and sat down on his bed.

"I'm hoping you would be willing to escort my daughter back and forth from work, with the wagon of course."

"I don't have a problem with that."

"No, I don't suppose you would. However, if I may be so forward, I've seen how you look at my daughter. And I know you have feelings for her."

Wyatt felt the heat rise on the back of his neck.

"That, son—" Jackson pointed to Wyatt's neck "—is my problem. I'm not here to force you to state your intentions, nor am I here to request formal courtship. I know how people will perceive it if you and she are together every day."

"Yes, sir. But you can't afford to have Ben miss school, and your other daughters are too young to be of much help for Mercy's protection. I understand. I will protect Mercy and her honor. Of that, you can be certain. I am no longer a young man whose passions flame so easily. You have no need to worry."

Jackson looked down at his lap. "I appreciate your honor and—" Jackson's gaze caught Wyatt's again "—I do trust you, sir."

"Thank you. That means a lot to me. I'd be happy to escort Mercy to and fro. Do you feel the need to speak with Robbie's father?"

"Not yet. I will if he approaches again, but Ben seems to think that he won't. He also said there was a definite change in his demeanor once you spoke to him. Did you notice that, as well?"

"Yes, sir. He seemed to dislike me. I can't honestly say why. Then again, if he has his heart set on Mercy and is aware that I've been about, he might see me as potential competition for Mercy's heart." *And he wouldn't be wrong.*

"Perhaps, but the entire business is a bit odd, don't you think? He has no words with Mercy except to tell her that she would make a good wife, after a couple years ago commenting how she would make a horrible wife."

"How are the Brown's financials?"

"Fine, as far as I can tell. Robbie isn't the oldest son,

though, and he's been a bit of a troublemaker in the past. I simply don't know what is happening, but I believe it will be necessary to protect Mercy at all costs, in spite of the likely black eye from gossips."

"I will do all that is necessary to protect her honor. I promise."

Jackson smiled. "I know you will, son. Or I'll hang your hide out for tanning."

Wyatt chuckled. "And I believe you might just do that, sir."

"You can count on it." Jackson gave a quiet laugh.

"Shall I ask to court her? Would that help?"

Jackson's laughter ceased. "Only if you are serious. I want to protect her heart, as well. You're a seagoing man. Your life is on the sea, not planted on solid ground."

"I was thinking...." What was he thinking? A courtship of convenience? No, that was not an honorable way to live either. "Forgive me. I wasn't really thinking the ramifications through."

Jackson stood. "I had similar thoughts, as well. So I'll not judge you, son." He clapped a hand on Wyatt's shoulder. "Thank you, Wyatt. I appreciate your help."

Wyatt could feel his chest swell. Twice in one day he'd been of value and worth to others, and it felt good. "You're welcome, sir."

"I'll send Mercy in so she can tell you her schedule."

"That would be fine, sir."

Ten minutes later, there was a gentler knock on his door. "Come in, Mercy."

"Papa said you'll be escorting me to and from work." She looked down at her shoes.

"Yes. Is that all right with you?"

She looked up to him with those wonderful blue

eyes. His heart beat more rapidly. It was the first time they'd been alone in over a week. Jackson Hastings's awareness of his children and those around him was very intuitive. "Are you certain you want to do this?"

He hopped forward. "Yes, I'd be honored."

She reached up, then obviously thought better of it and returned her arms to her sides. Not that Wyatt would have minded being touched by her. "Thank you. Personally, I'm not concerned but…"

Wyatt smiled. "But your father thinks it is best. I tend to agree with him. There was something in Robbie's eyes."

"You saw that, too?"

"Yes. When did you see it?"

"The day he came over and asked… correction…ordered me to court him. I have no interest in being that kind of a wife."

"No, I suspect not." He grinned.

"I suppose you think a wife should stay in her place and be told what to do by her husband?"

Wyatt attempted to raise his hands in surrender. "No, I didn't say or even mean to imply such a thing. I don't know you all that well, Mercy, but I do know that you would want to be an equal partner in a marriage. And I do know you wouldn't have trouble submitting to your husband, as I've seen you submit to your parents."

She relaxed. "Thank you. That has been my biggest grief. Folks not understanding that you can have free will but also submit. Father didn't raise no fool."

"No, he didn't." Wyatt turned and sat down on his bed. "Why don't you sit down and tell me about your schedule this week."

Mercy sat down on the couch, and Wyatt watched with fascination. He enjoyed the way she moved, the smile in her eyes, her delicate chin and... He cleared his throat. She began sharing the details of her schedule.

"I'll be up and ready. I wish I could help hook up the wagon."

"Ben's going to do that before he goes to school. In fact, Father is thinking we could take all of them to school in the morning."

"Anything you need done, I'm honored to help. I don't mind telling you, it has been hard to simply sit and be useless. In fact, I've been given two jobs today. Benjamin will be shrimping tonight, and I'll be cleaning them."

"Oh, how wonderful," she chuckled.

Wyatt laughed along with her. He felt at peace whenever she was near. "I know how to handle shrimp. I've done my share over the years."

"I suppose living on a ship does mean you'll have had your fair share of seafood."

"Some, but when you're transporting cargo, the faster you deliver, the better the profit. Of course, when you're under sail and the wind dies, you have little to do but hang out a fishing pole."

"I can't imagine. Do you lose much cargo when that happens?"

"Fortunately for Captain Nickerson, the cargo on the worst of those voyages was lumber and none perishable. We seldom dealt with food items. Too risky for profit. Which is why I was intending to buy a steam yacht. I'll be able to sail during strong winds and use steam power when the winds are low. It's the best of both worlds. Or rather, it was the best of both worlds." Wyatt sighed. It was hard to put aside his dream.

"Perhaps Sheriff Bower will have success."

Wyatt shook his head no. "I'm afraid not. He'll still

keep an ear to the ground, as they say, but he doesn't hold out much hope after all this time. It doesn't only affect me. It also affects James Earl, and his family, as well. They were planning on moving to Texas with the sale of the boat."

"Which makes little sense to me," Mercy offered. "Wouldn't he want to sail the boat to Texas, then sell it?"

Wyatt couldn't figure that out, either. Perhaps Sheriff Matt Bower was a little too quick to rule out James Earl. After all, he was the only one apart from the bank manager who'd known what kind of money he'd have on him. "I had similar thoughts, but Sheriff Bower doesn't feel he's a suspect."

"Maybe Sheriff Bower is allowing old family friends to impede his judgment." Mercy's eyes widened. "I'm sorry. I shouldn't have said that out loud. It is bad enough I would think such a thing, let alone speak it."

"Don't fret. I won't say anything to anyone. Not knowing people around here, I don't know if I truly trust anyone."

"Sheriff Bower has never given anyone cause for concern, but it does seem odd he can't find the men behind the robbery."

"I'm afraid he believes that the robbers were sailors and hightailed it out of port. I doubt he was able to search every vessel, and they could have been safely aboard a ship while I was still lying on the side of the road. Sheriff didn't even know about the crime until the tide had already gone out."

Mercy inhaled with enough strength to raise her shoulders. "He's probably right, unfortunately. I'm so sorry for your loss."

"I'm trying to give it over to God. It's hard to put aside your plans and dreams. Harder still to have them ripped from your hands. But the Bible speaks of the Lord putting things to right if you lean on Him."

"Romans 8:28. 'And we know all things work together for good to them that love God, to them who are called according to his purpose.'"

"Exactly the verse I had in mind. Although I admit it is a very difficult verse to swallow when life seems to be hitting you hard in the solar plexus. I have yet to see how the Lord will work this out for good when the thieves have gotten away with it, and I've lost the ability to buy my ship."

Mercy stood and walked over to him. She gently grasped his shoulder, "I can't answer that, Wyatt, but we do have to trust God."

He captured her hand with his. "I'm trying." He kissed the top of her hand. "I'll see you in the morning."

Her cheeks flamed. He hadn't meant to be so intimate. He'd wanted to thank her for her compassion. Perhaps her father had reason to be concerned about Mercy's honor in his presence. *Father, help me be the man Mercy needs.*

"Good night, Wyatt."

Mercy tossed and turned all night. It wasn't the first night's sleep she'd lost since finding Wyatt Darling on the side of the road and, more than likely, wouldn't be the last. They had fewer than thirty days left before he sat sail for the North and out of her life completely. Then she could sleep again, she hoped.

Washed and dressed for the day, Mercy went down the stairs. "Good morning, Mother. Anything I can help you with?" On the table, spread out before her mother, were eggs, bacon and biscuits.

"I'm fine. Your sisters said you kept them up half

the night. What was that about?" Rosemarie Hastings didn't beat around the bush when it came to finding out what was happening with her children.

"I'm sorry. I didn't realize I kept them awake. I'll be more careful in the future."

"That isn't telling me what was keeping you up all night."

"Nothing really."

"Is it this nonsense with Robbie Brown? I'll go over to his mother today and have some words with her."

Mercy sat down at the table and filled her plate. "It will be all right."

"I'm relieved Mr. Darling will be escorting you today. Taking the children to school will also give you chaperones for half the trip."

It wasn't really half the trip, but Mercy wouldn't argue with her mother. She knew her parents' concern about honor and respect in the community. She wouldn't fight them on this point. And she'd do her part, keeping a basket between the two of them while they rode on the front seat of the wagon.

"Good morning, Rosemarie, what a wonderful spread this morning." Wyatt shuffled in and sat down at the table. He'd been coming in for his meals for the past three days. Mercy smiled, then looked down at her plate.

"Momma! Bessie lost my book."

"Did not."

"Did, too. I lent it to you last night and you can't find it." Amy placed her hands on her hips.

"Girls, I won't have you squabbling in my house," Rosemarie warned. Mercy knew that tone. She'd learned very young you obeyed Mother when she used it.

"Yes, ma'am," Amy and Bessie said in unison.

"Now, Bessie, where were you reading the book last night?" Mother asked.

"On the sofa." Bessie answered.

"Amy, check under the cushions. Your father carried your sister to bed last night."

"Yes, ma'am."

"Bessie, sit down and eat while I fix your hair."

"Yes, ma'am."

Mercy caught Wyatt out of the corner of her eye. He held back a grin. Mercy cleared her throat to keep from laughing.

"JoJo's hooked up to the wagon. I need to change, then I'll be ready for school. Maman, may I take a plate with me?" Benjamin said as he walked into the kitchen, to the sink and rinsed his hands.

"I'll fix it right up for you, son."

"Thanks." Benjamin ran up the stairs two at a time.

"Found it!" Amy came running to the table and sat down. A farmhouse breakfast had a lot of food, and each person ate as they came in from their morning chores. By now, Father would have come in, eaten and returned to the barn. Mother finished brushing Bessie's hair, then filled a plate for Ben.

Mercy finished her eggs and brought her plate to the sink. Putting on her apron, she washed the few dishes in the sink and waited for Ben to come down. Wyatt's plate was passed over to her. She quickly washed it. Done, she set the apron aside and headed out to the wagon. Wyatt hobbled along behind her, as did Bessie, then Amy. Ben came, flinging his book bag over his shoulder and holding his breakfast plate steady with the other hand. "Thanks, Maman," he called out as he stepped down the back stairs.

Mother stood on the porch and watched them load into the wagon. "You girls behave yourselves today."

"Yes, ma'am."

Everyone said their goodbyes and Wyatt tapped the reins. JoJo's bridle and other equipment jangled. "I'm so excited." Bessie beamed. "We don't have to walk to school anymore."

"Don't get too used to this, Bessie. We'll only be doing it for this week."

"Well of course, silly. School gets out the end of this week."

Mercy laughed, as did Wyatt and the rest. They made their way to the school with light chatter. Benjamin managed to eat his breakfast and left his plate behind. Wyatt guided the wagon back toward the port and the various inns Mercy did the laundry for. At the back-door of the Tropical Breezes, she found Grace Martin waiting for them.

"Hi." Grace stepped forward. "I hope you don't mind, but I'd love to tag along with you again."

Mercy glanced back at Wyatt. "That would be fine. Mr. Darling, this is my good friend, Mrs. Martin."

"Pleasure to meet you." Wyatt gave a slight nod of the head.

"It is good to meet you, as well, Mr. Darling. I'm glad you are feeling better. We've been praying for your speedy recovery."

"Thank you."

Mercy excused herself and ran through the backdoor with the linens for the inn. She picked up the soiled laundry and replenished the shelves with the clean. Outside, she found Grace sitting on the bench seat of the wagon, along with Wyatt. "Where to next, my lady?" Wyatt gave a bow of the head.

"Je vous remercie, M. Darling. Beach Front Inn."

"Pardon, Je ne parle pas beaucoup français."

"And I don't speak any. What are you saying, Mercy?"

Mercy chuckled as she loaded up the wagon and climbed up to join Grace and Wyatt. "To the Beach Front Inn, *s'il vous plaît.*"

"Comme vous le souhaitez, Madame." Wyatt turned toward Grace and winked. "As you wish, my lady."

The crack of a gun rang through the air.

Chapter 7

Wyatt protected the ladies with his left arm, pushing them lower on the bench seat, and raised his head to see where the shots had come from. Over the years, he'd learned a gunshot didn't necessarily mean someone was in danger. A pile of men appeared outside the tavern. He watched for a moment longer as they manhandled a drunken individual off toward the sheriff's office. He sat up, raising his arm. "It's all clear. I'd say someone partook of the spirits."

Grace straightened her bonnet. Mercy's blue eyes widened. She squared her shoulders. "The Beach Front Inn is two blocks over and south a couple more."

Understanding his cue, he tapped the reins and led JoJo down the appropriate street. Grace wrung her hands in her lap for a moment. "It is a good thing Father was not down here. He'd never let me work for you."

"In all my days, that has never happened while I've

been in town." Mercy reached over and grabbed her girlfriend's hand.

Father? Didn't Mercy introduce her as Mrs.? Wyatt nodded and said hello to a few of the people who acknowledged him. He recognized some of their faces, but their names escaped him. Perhaps it was a good thing that Mrs. Martin was accompanying them this morning.

Wyatt finished the errands with Mercy and Grace and drove them back to the ranch. The ladies went to work, and Wyatt found his way to his room, where he picked up a book he'd begun reading last night. Beside that book lay another, which he hadn't realized was in French. It was clear that a third of the family library were books written in French. He'd learned that Rosemarie Hastings was of French descent and her family came to America just before she was born. But it was unique for Mercy to be so fluent in a foreign tongue.

He thought back on his ride with Jackson Hastings. He admired him. He took great care of his land, his stock and his employees. The sharecroppers he met on the ranch were well fed and seemed to have respect from Jackson. Jackson had adjusted from slave owner to employer well. Wyatt had come across far too many who hadn't made the adjustment and lost most of their family lands. His own father worked the land himself with the help of his wife and children. However, the size of the property was a fraction of what Jackson Hastings owned.

"Wyatt." Jackson called his name and a knock sounded on his door.

"Come in." Wyatt closed the book, keeping his forefinger in the place.

"Forgive the intrusion, but I was wondering if you saw any signs of Robbie Brown this morning?"

"No, sir."

Jackson nodded. "Good, good. Perhaps she is safe but I still feel it best…"

"It is not an imposition. I'm honored to escort her. Not to mention, it gives me something to do. There is nothing worse than a man feeling useless."

Jackson rubbed his chin. "You know I might be able to give you some small tasks. Several pieces of my equipment need to be polished or oiled. I'm certain Rosemarie would love to have some of her brass and silver polished."

Wyatt chuckled. "I haven't polished silver since I was a boy, but I'd be happy to do it. As for brass, I polished my fair share on board. I also make some mighty fine knots and splice rope with ease."

"Now that is something I could use." Jackson went on to explain his various needs with regard to rope, cattle and the ranch. Within ten minutes, Wyatt was out of his room, following Jackson around the barn with a list that would keep him busy for days.

"I appreciate the help." Jackson held out his hand.

Wyatt leaned on his crutch and shook it. "Pleasure to be useful. It will help me feel good about earning my keep."

"We won't go over that old discussion again. But I'm glad we could find something useful for you to do. Pace yourself. Don't try and get it done in one day."

Wyatt laughed. "Don't believe that is possible." Busywork ran a ship and kept it running in tip-top condition. Most of the sailors understood that. Occasionally, he'd run across one who didn't. And with some good, hard work, they would learn to appreciate it. If they didn't, they were let go at the next port. Wyatt smiled, thinking back on the days when he thought himself too good for busywork. The scars on his back started to itch. There was nothing like a humbling keelhauling or being stranded on an island with your men to show you differently. Wyatt rolled his shoulders and went to work. Jackson provided the brass polish and oils for the leather and metal parts of the harnesses.

"I'll send young Moses over to help run to and fro."

"I can manage."

Jackson placed a hand on his shoulder. "I know you can. However, Moses, Sr. and his family can use a little extra, and I'm trying to encourage Moses, Jr. to seek an education to help his family. Anything you can say to the boy to help that along would be appreciated."

"Yes, sir. I understand." Wyatt had met Moses on more than one occasion and knew the part the young boy had played in helping fetch Dr. Peck. But to hear Jackson Hastings encouraging his former slaves to seek an education... Well, that was not typical.

Jackson laughed. "No, apparently you don't, but I don't have time to explain it to you right now."

"Sorry, sir. I didn't realize my confusion showed."

"I get reactions like that all the time. Excuse me, but I have some business I need to tend to."

Wyatt nodded. He looked over the array of items on the workbench and realized he couldn't stand for very long. He'd need a high stool of some sort to get this work done. He started to search the barn....

The next three days went the same. Wyatt drove the wagon. They dropped the children off at school and met up with Grace outside Tropical Breezes Inn. To be so close to him and not have any moment for private conversation drove Mercy to seek him out. Seeing an opportunity after she finished her chores, she slipped into the barn and found him toiling. "What are you working on?"

Wyatt jumped.

"Sorry." Wyatt moaned and reached for his crutches. "You startled me."

"I'm sorry. Did you hurt your leg?"

"Some. It will be fine. I can't make sudden moves without noticing it." Wyatt sat back down.

Mercy controlled an impulse to reach over and rub his shoulders and set his muscles at ease.

"I understand you and Benjamin will be leaving in a couple days to harvest salt."

"Yes, we'll camp on the beach for two or three days, boil down the seawater and harvest as many barrels as possible. Have you seen the shed where Father ages his beef?"

"Only from a distance. It's huge—the size of a barn. Why so large?"

"The meat is more tender and he can sell choice cuts for their chefs to the large hotels. It takes a bit more work, but the pay is worth it. And the family benefits from having some of the best beef in town as our everyday dinner."

"I won't deny that. I've seldom had a steak as tender as what I've had here."

"Wyatt, may I ask you a personal question?"

He put the brass lantern down. "You may ask."

"What happened to your family?"

He closed his eyes and eased out a breath. "I was thirteen, and my parents, brothers and sisters were heading from the Cape to Boston. It's a short sail from Provincetown. In 1853, a tremendous squall hit Cape Cod. Twenty ships were sunk inside Provincetown Harbor alone. Unfortunately, my parents and siblings were farther out to sea when the storm hit and were some of the casualties. I'd stayed home overseeing the live-stock. When I received word that my family had died, I boarded up the house and set sail with Captain Nick-erson."

"Have you ever been back?"

"I spent a couple of holidays with the Nickersons, but it was too painful to return to the house. By the time I was sixteen I stopped going to the Nickersons for the holidays. By the time I was eighteen, I was serving on other ships, and well, I haven't been home since."

"But you've decided to return home now, why?" She noticed the muscle in his jaw twitch.

"Because I have property there. I've let it be run by a caretaker and I've ignored it for too long. Captain Nick-erson has overseen the caretaker. The pain of my loss has kept me from returning. But it's time. In truth, it is well past time. It's a funny thing about the sea, you can avoid so many things simply working hard and stay-ing on board."

"I think I understand. Do you think God's used this horrible theft to stop you long enough for you to realize you've been running away from your past?"

Wyatt looked down at his lap. "You have a knack for coming straight to the point, don't you?"

"Sorry. It is a weakness. Forgive me for being for-ward."

Wyatt reached out and grabbed her hand. "No, don't apologize to me. You're probably right. I've had a lot of time to think. The first couple weeks, I was angry and so frustrated that I couldn't go out and find those men and get back my money. Living here with your family… Well, let's just say the Lord's been showing me some things I've been running from. And my family and estate is one of those things. I am the last Darling to carry on the legacy. We own prime property in Cotuit Port. It's been in my family for well over a hundred and fifty years. I've decided I'm not going to be the Darling who gives up that legacy."

"How will you pass that on if you don't intend to marry?" Mercy covered her mouth with her hands. Why was she so bold with this man?

Wyatt laughed out loud. "You are direct. I've only gotten as far as my need to return to the land. I haven't thought of the future. But you are right. If I'm to pass on this legacy, I shall need a family...."

"Forgive me."

"There is nothing to forgive." He stood with his crutches and went back to work.

He'd finally opened up a little to her. She wasn't about to push it. Tomorrow, Grace would not be joining them on their rounds. Mercy realized she was looking forward to no more school drop-offs and Grace not being with them. She reached over and tapped him on the back. She could feel the hard lump of his scar. She pulled her hand back. "I'll see you in the morning."

"Good night, Mercy."

"Good night, Wyatt."

The rest of the evening, Mercy thought back on the conversation in the barn. To lose all of his family in one day...how horrifying... She could understand his not wanting to return, but it had been nearly seventeen years. Then again, when he spoke of his family and the legacy of the land, there was a pride, a healthy pride, in him about his heritage.

She remembered the warmth of his touch on her skin. The hunger to wrap him in her arms and help soothe the pain away grew every moment she thought about it. She readied herself for bed. She would try to sleep as ramrod straight as possible in order to not pester her sisters, who were still giggling about no more school for the summer.

The next morning came with a groan. She hadn't slept well. Her sisters kept her up most of the night. She woke several times tangled up in the sheets from her own foolish dreams of wrapping herself in Wyatt's arms and kissing away his pain. The girls were sleeping sweetly. Mercy found her way to the bathroom and pumped cold water on her face. At least she could blame the girls for her lack of sleep this time, although it was only half-true.

She went down the stairs to find Benjamin eating his breakfast, proclaiming, "I'll be coming to town this morning with you."

"Oh?"

"Yes'm. We'll be taking the larger buggy. Father has a shipment that's come in."

"A shipment of what?"

"Axle grease."

"Axle grease? He didn't make his own?"

Ben shook his head and scarfed down some more of his hash brown potatoes. "Nope. He saw an advertisement and thought the price was right."

"It better be packed well. I can't afford to have axle grease on my clients' linens."

Ben stood up from the table, his mouth still full, and carried his plate to the sink. "With all this complaining, I'd think someone had her heart set on—"

Mother walked in. Ben stopped his teasing. "What's going on?"

"Rien, Maman," Mercy and Benjamin said in unison. Ben hurried out to prepare the wagon.

"Mercy?"

"Nothing, *Maman,* I promise."

"I'll let it drop this time, but I am not clueless."

"No, Mother, you are not. The girls kept me up half the night giggling about not having any more school for the year."

"*Oui,* but I saw you and how you behaved last evening. Are you and Mr...." Her mother's words trailed off as Wyatt stumbled in through the backdoor. "Good morning, Mr. Darling. Did you sleep well?"

"Fairly. Mercy, I'll need to stay in town in order for Dr. Peck to remove my cast this morning. Benjamin says he's coming to town with us. Can you leave me at the doctor's? I can try to negotiate a ride home later with someone."

Mercy nodded. "Of course." She didn't want to see his leg without a cast again.

Wyatt sat down. He knew he was interrupting a conversation between mother and daughter and prayed he was not the cause of it. Last night had been the worst since the accident. He couldn't sleep. He kept remembering Mercy's delicate touch. Not to mention the fact that if he were to continue the legacy of his family, he would need to have one of his own. And avoiding the very thought of Mercy Hastings being his wife, to continue his lineage, had kept him up all night.

He sat down at the table and ate his breakfast as quickly as possible. Mercy sat down and ate hers. Rosemarie joined them, as well, and poured herself a cup of hot tea.

"Very good breakfast as usual, Rosemarie. Thank you. You are spoiling me. I may never want to go back to sea."

"You are most kind, Mr. Darling."

Wyatt noted the formal use of his name. Something had changed. Had Mercy told her parents of his reaching out for her hand? He glanced at Mercy. Her dazzling blue eyes sparkled. A gentle pink infused her cheeks. He turned his focus on the plate of food in front of him. This was no time to speculate and no time to get lost in thoughts that were beyond his ability to even grasp. He had his own life to live, and his future was limited at the moment. No man should consider marrying when he didn't know if he could provide for a wife or whether he would be going back to sea. Granted, if he sailed the East Coast, a wife wouldn't be out of the question. Then again, some of the most lucrative journeys took six months or more.

He forked the scrambled eggs and kept his mouth full instead of voicing his inner thoughts.

"Mercy, would you stop by Rachael Ward's dress shop for me on your way home? I'm in need of some supplies. I've written a list for you."

"I'd be happy to." Mercy ate a lighter than normal breakfast this morning, Wyatt noted.

Breakfast done, he worked his way to the wagon, where Benjamin stood waiting, holding JoJo's bridle. "When do you and Mercy leave for the salt harvest?"

"Tomorrow. Would you like to join us?"

"No, beach sand and a cast don't mix."

"I reckon you're right." Benjamin climbed up on the bench. The wagon was fully loaded with clean linens. Mercy worked hard and she ran a tight business.

"I understand you harvest salt once a year?"

"Most of the time, that's true. Once in a while, it is twice a year. There are advantages to doing it in the summer when there are longer days, but there are also advantages of doing it in the winter when it is cooler. Overall, the summer wins because the sun helps to evaporate some of the water."

"We didn't have much need of making salt on board a ship. And we could purchase it easily enough. From what I understand, you use a fair amount of it for your father's meat business."

Benjamin nodded. Mercy came out from the house and joined them on the bench seat of the wagon. Wyatt took the reins, then thought better of it and handed them to Benjamin, who sat in the middle. "Here you go."

Ben smiled. "Thanks." Ben jiggled the reins and JoJo lunged forward. Wyatt sat back and kept his gaze from Mercy. They were entering dangerous territory, and both of them knew it. He couldn't deny his attraction. He was old enough to ignore it and focus on what really mattered, getting well and moving on with his life.

An hour later, he sat in the doctor's office hanging on to the examination bedframe with all of his might. The pain that surged from his leg while the doctor unpacked the wound had him seeing stars—in spite of the pain medication the doctor had given him.

"I'm sorry, Mr. Darling," Dr. Peck apologized. "The infection is much better, and I am certain you will not lose your leg. However, I need to do some surgery. I'm going to put you under with some chloroform. I might have to give you a second dose while I'm operating. You would be unable to sit still because of the level of pain."

"No pain sounds just fine at the moment," Wyatt said through gritted teeth.

The doctor's door flung open with a bang. "Dr. Peck, can I watch?" Benjamin Hastings stood in the doorway.

"Where's your sister?" Wyatt demanded. "You're supposed to be watching over her."

"She's fine. I left her at the dressmaker's shop."

"Benjamin Hastings, go to your sister at once, and I shall not tell your father of your lack of concern on her behalf."

Ben paled and turned to leave. "Sorry, you're right, Wyatt." He slipped out the door just as Wyatt noticed the sweet smell of chloroform hitting his nostrils. "Relax, Mr. Darling, the boy will take care of his sister. Now count for me."

"One…" Then there was nothing. No care, no thought, nothing.

Chapter 8

Mercy gathered the items her mother had ordered and placed them in a small basket to take home. Inside the store she felt safe. Outside, on the sidewalk, everyone seemed to be a suspect. She closed her eyes for a moment and relaxed. Robbie hadn't harmed her. Why was she so worried? Perhaps all the protection that Wyatt offered and her father's overprotective nature were more the cause than the actual threat. She placed the basket in the wagon and walked down to Monsieur Franc's shop where one could purchase items from France. Inside the shop she found the latest novels. She browsed through the assortment and her eyes landed on *The Mystery of Orcival,* by Emile Gaboriau. Perhaps a real mystery might help suspend her foolish fears.

Benjamin bolted through the door. "There you are."

"What's the matter?"

"You mean, besides the fact that you weren't in the dress shop any longer?"

"Don't you start, too." Mercy paid for her purchase and left the store with her brother on her heels.

"I already received a stern warning from Mr. Darling. How long do we need to protect you like this?" Benjamin came up beside her and stuffed his hands in his pockets.

"I don't know. I didn't feel safe walking out of the dress shop. It's discouraging. It is not good to live like this. I'm going to have a word with Father."

Benjamin raised his hands. "Look, I saw Robbie's eyes, and he didn't look right, but I'm beginning to think he won't hurt you."

"I don't think he will, either. Let's hope Father sees it that way as well. I can't imagine how many bodyguards he'll require at the beach."

Benjamin climbed up on the wagon. "I hadn't thought about that. I think you and I can handle it. But…"

"But there's been not a sign of Robbie since you last spoke with him. I believe the threat is over. Perhaps we can hire young Moses to join us. Another set of hands won't hurt."

Ben smiled. "Nope, they would probably help. What about the girls?"

"Do you want to play nursemaid to those two all day?"

"Nope, you're right. Moses it is."

Mercy grabbed the reins and led JoJo back home. "I've got a lot of work to do today. Can you pack up the supplies for the salt harvest?"

Ben shrugged. "I guess."

"What's the matter?"

Ben gnawed his inner cheek. "Are you in love with Wyatt?"

"No! Why do you ask?"

Ben shrugged his shoulders. "I don't know. I heard Mother and Father talking. They are worried you might be falling in love with him. They don't think it's a good thing that he's ten years older than you. On the other hand, they think he's a good man. What do you think?"

"I think you've been eavesdropping a bit too much. I like Mr. Darling well enough, but we have not had any discussions revolving around a relationship." Her dreams were another matter all together, but she wasn't about to tell her brother those, especially a younger brother.

"I'm concerned how Father will be able to run the ranch if I leave to go to college. And if you get married to Mr. Darling, you won't be helping with the ranch. Amy and Bessie are of little help."

"Have you told Maman and Papa that you'd like to become a doctor?"

"Not exactly. I was hoping to go in to tell them last night when I heard them discussing you and Mr. Darling."

That explains Mother's behavior this morning.

"I really like medicine. Everything I've been learning from Dr. Peck encourages me to want to learn more. I've spoken with my teacher and he's putting together a course load for me next year that will secure the proper classes for college and a degree in medicine."

"And this is what you were going to speak with Maman and Papa about last night?"

"Yes, but as I said…"

Mercy held up her hand. She didn't want to be reminded of what her parents were discussing. Their conversations went far deeper than any she and Wyatt had had.

They rode in silence the rest of the way home. She

needed to have a word with her mother or Father. They shouldn't be so concerned with regard to her and Wyatt. Then again, her overactive imagination while she slept... Perhaps they had a point. *The question still remains, am I falling in love with him or is it my desire to help him?* Or was it the bond she felt having been his rescuer. She'd been debating that point for weeks to no avail. Mercy sighed.

"I know, I know. I'll talk with them soon. Perhaps after the salt harvest."

Mercy retraced her conversation with Benjamin. *What is he talking about? Oh, yes. Studying medicine. His need for schooling and his need to tell our parents.* "We'll talk about it while we're harvesting so you can approach Maman and Papa with a constructive plan. Do you know what the cost of your education will be?"

"No. It depends on where I attend college. Dr. Peck has written to a few schools for me so I can present some figures to Maman and Papa."

At the house they parted ways, Benjamin on to his chores and Mercy on to washing the linens for her customers. Around dinner time, her mother approached. "Mercy, may I have a moment of your time?"

Wyatt awoke groggy. He didn't like the chloroform. Then again, he didn't like the pain he'd experienced the last time Dr. Peck had to cut out some of the wound.

"Welcome back. How are you feeling?"

"A little dry in the mouth and a little nauseated."

Dr. Peck scribbled some notes down. "Not to be concerned. That is normal. Let's give it an hour or two and then I can order a cab for you."

"What did you find?"

"Your leg is healing quite well. The surgery I did today will help the wound heal. I removed some splinters of bone that were floating toward the surface. The stitches from the surgery will be ready to come off in a week, but they can stay on a little bit longer until I remove the cast and replace it again. You'll note that the cast goes over your knee this time. There's a slight bend to the knee, for easier walking. You've been moving around a bit too much with the shorter cast, so this will keep the leg more stable as you continue to get around."

"I'm trying to stay put," Wyatt said defensively.

"You're fine. I know the temptation to do more is a part of your anxiousness to recover and get back to work." Dr. Peck stood up from his desk. "Speaking of which, Sheriff Bower came by. He said to let you know that there is no news. He'd like a detailed description of your money belt."

Wyatt nodded. He was almost getting used to hearing bad news from the sheriff. He and Dr. Peck continued with some light conversation until Wyatt's eyes started to droop. He yawned. "Pardon me."

"Nonsense. I'm surprised you were talkative. Rest, let the body heal itself."

Wyatt closed his eyes and let sleep overtake him. He was in and out over the next couple of hours. Jack Hastings came in and offered a ride back to the ranch. When they arrived, the ranch was alive with activity. Wyatt sequestered himself in his room. Mercy and Benjamin were packing a wagon for the salt harvest. The girls were running about enjoying their first day of summer vacation. Jackson and Jack were busy, planning to migrate the herd to the southern pastures. Rosemarie was involved with dinner preparations, besides putting food together for Mercy and Benjamin.

Wyatt closed his eyes and fell asleep again, wondering just how powerful was that chloroform?

A gentle knock at the door mustered him from his slumber. "Wyatt," Mercy's soothing voice called.

He grabbed his crutches and came to the door. "Hi, how can I help you?"

"Dinner is ready."

"Thank you. Tell your mother I'll be up in a few minutes. I'd like to freshen up a bit."

Mercy nodded. She reached out for his forearm, then pulled her hand away. "I hope Dr. Peck gave you good news."

"He did. Thank you."

Mercy smiled. His stomach flipped. He steeled his heart. He couldn't let himself sail that current of thought.

"I'll tell Mother to expect you."

Wyatt thanked her and before his thoughts could betray him further, he closed the door. He shuffled over to the commode and poured some fresh water into the bowl. After a quick once-over, he made his way over to the house and up the rear stairs. He turned and scanned the area surrounding them. Between the trees, he could see the pasture. Around the house, they had kept as many trees as possible, providing shade from the hot Florida sun.

Inside, everyone was seated at the table. Wyatt took his seat and placed his crutches on the floor. "Everything looks scrumptious this evening, Mrs. Hastings."

"Thank you, Mr. Darling." The formality of the names caused Wyatt to question if he were overextending his time with the Hastings. Perhaps he should take a room in the city.

"Let's pray." Jackson bowed his head. Everyone followed suit. Wyatt clasped his own hands and silently prayed to not be a burden on this very loving and giving family. After Jackson finished the prayer it was a free-for-all. In reality, it was a well-orchestrated dinner table. They all took what was in front of them and passed it on to the person on their left. Within short order, all the items on the table had made it onto a plate or at least around the table.

Today's fare had everything Wyatt enjoyed. He bit into a croissant and moaned with pleasure. "Excellent, Mrs. Hastings, as always."

Jackson chuckled. "Rosemarie won me over with her cooking, especially the French pastries and sauces. Her mother was an excellent cook and my Rosemarie learned well. Jackson reached over and squeezed his wife's hand. Wyatt cast his gaze away. Memories flooded in of times at his parents' table, watching the love between them.

"Mr. Darling, are you all right?" Bessie asked.

Wyatt smiled. "Just fine, sweetheart. I was remembering when I was around your age and sharing a meal with my family."

"Why'd they die?" Bessie asked.

"Bessandra Elizabeth!" Jackson and Rosemarie said in unison.

All eyes glared at Bessie. She shrank back in her chair.

"It's all right. My family was lost at sea when I was thirteen. I stayed home to watch the farm, or I would have been lost, too."

"I'm sorry you lost all your family. What do you do at Christmas?" Bessie continued with the innocence of a young child.

Wyatt chuckled. "I haven't had a family Christmas or

any holiday since I was a boy. Captain Nickerson took me to his home a few times, but it wasn't the same. So I stopped accepting his offers by the time I was sixteen."

"Consider this an open invitation if you're in port during the holidays. You can join the family," Jackson offered as he forked his steak.

Wyatt didn't want to say no but knew in his heart he would have the same trouble as he'd had when he was a boy, with all the childhood memories flooding back in. "Thank you. I appreciate it."

He caught a glimpse of Mercy before he trained his eyes back on his own plate.

Mercy sliced the steak on her plate and forced her gaze away from Wyatt. After dinner her mother and she were destined to have the personal and private conversation she'd been hoping to avoid. But there was no avoiding the truth. Wyatt Darling captivated her. As much as she'd hoped it was just a passing interest, her thoughts, her dreams all attested to the fact that she'd developed great affection for Mr. Darling. *Perhaps if I keep using his proper name, even in my personal thoughts, I'd have more control over them....* She glanced back at Wyatt. *Perhaps not.*

He continued to eat his meal without so much as a glance in her direction. *Could it be that he is not attracted to me? Of course, I am nearly ten years younger.* Mercy concentrated on her steak, her appetite all but gone. It wasn't right to not clear her plate. She would sit here until her entire meal was through.

One by one, everyone left the table until only Mercy remained. She slumped back in her chair.

"Mercy, come take a walk with me." Her mother

stood in the doorway of the dining room and removed her apron.

Mercy glanced at her plate, pushed it away and stood up. "That would be nice."

Mother smiled. Mercy smiled in return and the weight she'd been carrying seemed to lift off her shoulders. Her parents had always been fair. She couldn't imagine them being anything but at this moment. "Come, *ma* chérie. We have much to discuss, no?"

"Oui, ma maman." Her mother led her out the back-door and down the path toward the river. They sat on the small bridge and dangled their bare toes in the water. "We should have brought our bathing clothes."

"Then we would have your sisters with us. No, it is better that we are alone now. I reckon you know what we need to discuss."

Mercy nodded in affirmation.

"Then perhaps it would be best if you told me what you are feeling."

"*Ma maman,* where should I begin? I do care for Mr. Darling but we have not spoken any words apart from general conversation."

"And yet you have great affection for him?"

"It consumes me. Consumes is too strong a word. I think about him, pray for him constantly. And occasionally I wonder what it might be like to be his wife." Mercy's heart raced. The admission was more than she had admitted to herself.

"Ah, so you tossed and turned because of these thoughts, no?"

"Oui. But I don't believe he cares for me in the same manner."

"You might be surprised, *ma chérie.* I have seen how he watches you when he doesn't believe anyone is looking. I know this look. I have seen it in your father when we fell in love many years ago, and I have seen it with your brother and his wife. Now it appears you may have found the one who is meant for you. My concern is his past life. He's been on his own for many years. He has not had a loving family to help him while he was not yet a man."

"I know very little about his past. I knew about his family but only a few hours before he mentioned it to all of us. The scars on his back…"

"The what? Where?"

Mercy felt her cheeks flame. "The first day when he came to stay with us. I saw scars on his back. I have seen slaves with scars from whippings, but I have never seen a scar like that before. It went straight down his back and must have been at least a couple inches wide."

"Oh, my. On the docks I have seen some men who have had scars like that. It came from an old practice on ships. When someone would not obey, they were keelhauled."

Mercy's eyes widened. She'd read about such horrible ordeals. "You mean someone tied a rope around him and dragged him under the ship from bow to stern?"

"That would be my guess." Her mother paused. "And that is where your father's and my concern comes from. From everything we've seen from Mr. Darling, he seems to be an honorable man. He said he did not partake of the spirits, and yet someone had to have known he had so much money on him at the time they beat him."

"But Wyatt has done nothing to show a reason for distrust. He has earned the right to be a captain of a ship. Discipline and good character would be the requirement for such a position. Would they not?"

"*Oui, ma chérie.* I did not say these things to say they are true, just that they are questions your *père* and I have. You are right, he has shown himself to be a gentleman on more than one occasion but we…" Her mother paused. "But we are parents, and as parents, we are concerned. Perhaps it is not necessary, but it is how we feel."

"I think I understand."

"But these are not all the reasons I wanted to speak with you. I wanted to speak with you woman to woman about these desires and feelings. Perhaps I can help with how to manage them."

Mercy smiled. She loved her mother. Their conversation lingered until the sky was darkening. She'd been the one to help her through those dark days when the boys had said why they would not want her as a wife. It had been her mother who had encouraged her to be the woman God had designed her to be. She remembered the conversation with Robbie and how he viewed women, as if they were no better than slaves. And the War of Aggression was too new for people not to be unaware of the attitudes that still prevailed.

Her mind drifted over to Wyatt and their conversations. He never once thought of a woman as inferior. "Wyatt is not Robbie."

"No *ma chérie.* He is a much better man."

"*Oui.*"

"It is late. We shall talk more after you return from the salt harvest."

"*Merci beaucoup. Je t'aime, maman.*" Mercy reached over and hugged her mother.

Rosemarie kissed the top of Mercy's head. "*Je t'aime aussi.*"

* * *

The next morning, Wyatt watched as Mercy and Benjamin drove off toward the beach. A part of him wanted to be at her side to protect her. Another part knew that if he spent any more time with her he'd do something foolish, and he couldn't afford to change his plans. The question was, what were his plans? For years, he'd been so focused on owning his own vessel. Prior to the attack, he could have been hired as a captain without owning his own ship. He looked down at the plaster cast, still bright and clean. The doc was right, putting the cast over his knee meant he had less flexibility. Would he ever be able to walk again without the aid of a cane? The doctor seemed encouraged but...

He tossed the book over onto the small table. Frustration oozed from every pore. He wanted to do more. He couldn't even pursue his own attackers, not that he had the investigative skills, but still... He felt helpless. Recovering from the wounds on his back had taken less time. Over the years, his life had been in jeopardy on several occasions and each time he'd recovered and returned to his work. This time... Wyatt stood up on his good leg and hopped over to the bed. "I can't even kneel to pray."

"Forgive me, Lord. I'm in a sour disposition this morning. But I need Your strength, and help me find my purpose in life again."

The rap on his door was masculine, which meant it was Jack or Jackson.

Jack opened the door and smiled. "Morning, Wyatt." He was a couple of inches taller than his father but apart from that he appeared to be a younger version of the man.

"Come in." Wyatt shifted his weight, pivoted and sat down on the edge of his bed.

"I have a parcel here for you. It came this morning."

Wyatt took the large, thick envelope. "Thank you." He noted the return address. "Ah, I've been waiting on this."

"Then I'll bid you good day." Jack nodded and stepped out of the room, closing the door behind him.

Wyatt ripped open the envelope and scanned the pages. His hands started to shake. He'd had no idea how much wealth he had accumulated over the years. He wasn't a rich man, but...

He turned back the pages to the cover letter from Captain Nickerson and read it slowly.

Dear Wyatt,

It is good to hear from you, son. I was sorry to hear of your troubles in St. Augustine. But as you will see you have the funds to purchase the ship from your accounts up here.

I'm afraid I do have some bad news. My health is not what it was, and I am going to have to relinquish the oversight of your accounts. I am not as lively as I once was, and well, let's just say Alice is more than happy to have me home and focused on family. I shall oversee for as long as you need, but I trust you shall be able to take care of these matters on your own. It will mean you need to come north and visit your property at least once a year. I've enclosed Jason Smith's response to your letter, as well, since our letters arrived within days of one another.

Son, I understand the difficult position it is for you to return to your parents' home, but you're thirty years, and I believe it is time.

I have enclosed a check for two hundred dol-

lars, which should give you adequate funds for
a while. The banking information is included in
case you wish or need to transfer additional funds.
However, I have prayed about this matter, and I
really believe you should return to Cotuit Port and
oversee your property. Please understand your
caretaker has been doing an excellent job. You
are a man and should take full control of your
responsibilities.
Your friend and mentor,
John

Wyatt moved from the bed and reread Captain Nickerson's letter and went over all the detailed accountings
for the last fifteen years. Each year, Jason Smith had
made a profit. The first couple years, it was merely a
few hundred dollars. The farm must have been in quite
a state of disrepair, having lain idle for a while. As he
worked through the final pages of financial reports and
bank statements, Wyatt was overwhelmed by God's
provision.

He took in a deep pull of air and released it slowly.
A desire to run to the bank and cash the check took
root in the pit of his stomach. Another thought hit
him equally as hard. Would he be attacked again for a
couple hundred dollars? Did he trust the banker? The
sheriff? Admittedly, he did not. "Forgive me, Father.
I am afraid."

He thought back on his home in Cotuit Port, of the
past memories that were held there. Of the good times
and the horror of the day when Captain Nickerson re-
ported to him that all of his family had been lost. His
heart started to race. He took short, deep breaths. His
chest rose and fell with each one. His mind went back to

that moment when he was thirteen and overcome with anguish. "Dear God, I can't." He gripped the arms of the sofa and held on until his knuckles whitened, like lightning flashing before his eyes. He traveled back in time, to the horrific moment he'd been told his family had perished. His mind raced between the past and the present. He traveled to the deep moments of need to cling to the arms of the father and mother no longer able to embrace him. Back and forth his mind went, until he was weak and defenseless. He was alone, so utterly alone. He sat in another man's spare room unable to provide for himself. He glanced down at the sheets of paper. Well, not completely unable.

But he was alone. Even Captain Nickerson was stepping away from the oversight of his finances. Not that he didn't have a point. At thirty years of age, Wyatt was more than capable of taking care of his own properties. The problem was he didn't see it as his property, but his parents'. The facts were he was the oldest son and the farm would have been given to him after his parents retired or passed. *Why can't I face this, Lord? Why do I react like I'm a thirteen-year-old child when it comes to this?*

Mercy fed the fire while Benjamin carried another bucket of water to the salt pot. One thing was certain, you built up your arm and back muscles carrying ocean water to and fro to the kettle. The campfire had to be above the high-tide mark or else you could be flooded out when the tide came in. The tent was set up, the fires were burning and several gallons of water had been boiled off, leaving a slight skim of salt encrusted on the pot. Rather than take the time to remove the early crystals, they simply added more water. They would do this for a couple rounds before they would scrape the salt off the sides and bottom of the pot. They would repeat the process again and again until the barrels were full. Three days and many hours of backbreaking work lay between long hours with little to do.

Mercy sat down on the chair, which sunk deep into the sand, and stretched her legs out in front of her. She reached into her bag and pulled out the new novel she had purchased yesterday at Monsieur Franc's shop, *The Mystery of Orcival*.

"What do you have there?" Benjamin asked as he poured the water into the pot.

"A new mystery novel."

"French?"

"Oui."

Ben tossed the bucket to the side, checked the logs on the fire and settled down beside her. "I read French a lot better than I speak it."

"You'll be learning Latin if you become a doctor."

"Yeah, and I speak a little French and Spanish, so that ought to bode well with my studies."

"Did you speak with Maman and Papa?"

"No, I thought I'd wait. When we return I'll sit down with them."

"Did you get some figures with regard to the expenses for schooling?"

"Some." Benjamin sat down in the sand and leaned back on his elbows. "It will be expensive. I don't know how I'll be able to afford it. I'm certain Maman and Papa will try to help, but a part of me wants to be able to pay for my education on my own."

Ben had a strong work ethic. It came with being the children of Jackson and Rosemarie Hastings.

"The Medical College of Georgia in Augusta, Georgia, is the closest, and nonresidents are charged a hundred and fifty dollars per semester. But that is after I attend another college for at least two years with a science background. Then at Augusta I would need to attend for four years. Tuition alone is three hundred a year for four years for Medical School. That doesn't take into account housing and living expenses."

Mercy had that much in her savings. Would it be right to give her brother the money? Where would that leave her? Living with her parents for another six years, no doubt.

"Mercy? What's the matter?"

"Nothing. Sorry. You're correct, living expenses would be needed, as well. Where would you go for the first two years?"

"I have no idea. It seems so far off and I'm talking about the next seven to eight years of my life. That's nearly half my lifetime."

"True, little brother. If you really believe it is what you wish to do, money should not stop you."

Benjamin doodled in the sand for a moment. "What about what happened to Wyatt Darling? He saved for years, and in one horrific act, he lost everything. I wouldn't want to put that kind of burden on Maman and Papa. What if something happened to me? What if…?"

"Ben, you can't go about your life in fear. If I lived that way I wouldn't have my own business. I wouldn't have a sizable savings and a vision for my future."

"What is your future, Mercy? Do you see yourself getting married?"

Mercy swallowed the bitter taste that rose in her mouth.

"I'm sorry, I didn't mean to offend you. I know what

those men said and how horrible they were. What I was meaning to say was do you want to get married or do you prefer living independently."

Mercy raised her eyebrows.

"Oh, fiddlesticks, I'm not sayin' this right! Forget me asking."

Mercy laughed. "It's all right, Ben. I understand what you mean. And the answer is yes, I'd like to get married some day. But I won't be marrying someone like Robbie, who thinks of a wife as no more than a slave."

"Father doesn't treat Mother like that. He cherishes her, and they both work really hard."

"Yes, they do."

"Which is why I don't want to burden them with my education expenses. Perhaps I could go to sea like Wyatt and earn my money for college, then go on to medical school."

"Perhaps you should pray about it some more. God will grant a way if it is His desire for you to become a doctor."

Benjamin nodded. "You're right. I'm going to check on the fire. You can sit and relax for a bit, read your book."

"Thank you." Mercy leaned back in her chair, closed her eyes and prayed. Was she the answer to her brother's prayers? Had her savings been for him and not herself? Should she sacrifice it all for him? *Dear Lord, I need to know for certain if I should do this.*

After a few minutes of silence, Mercy opened her new novel and inhaled the fresh smell of ink and paper. She closed her eyes for a moment and soaked it all in. Then she began to read.

"Hello!" Billy Crabtree strode into their camp. Mercy's spine stiffened. All of her senses were on high alert.

"Billy? What brings you out here?"

"You," he answered and winked.

Chapter 9

Determined to rise above the suffocating images of the past, Wyatt grabbed his crutches and exited his room. The day was more than half over. He couldn't ride into town on a horse, but perhaps the Darlings would allow him the use of another of their wagons.

He scanned the yard and found Rosemarie hanging out the morning laundry, along with Grace Martin. Both seemed to be working at Mercy's job. "Mrs. Hastings, may I have a word with you?"

She pinned the last corner of the sheet she was hanging and wiped her hands on her apron. "What can I help you with, Mr. Darling?"

"I need to go to town. I'm wondering if I could borrow the wagon?"

Rosemarie turned toward Grace. "Would you be agreeable to Mr. Darling driving you back in to town?"

"That would be fine. Give me fifteen more minutes and I'll have the laundry hung."

"I do not wish to take you from your chores. I can manage on my own." He wasn't that much of an invalid that he needed a woman to escort him to town. "Forgive me, let me rephrase my needs. I am grateful to you and Mr. Hastings for your provisions for me, but I have procured some funds and I shall be securing some lodgings in town before I head back home to Cotuit Port."

"Oh…well…that is different. Let me get Jackson." Rosemarie Hastings marched over to the steel triangle, grabbed the rod and hammered out a signal. If her husband were in the upper pasture he would respond. Over the past several weeks, he'd seen how they communicated with this primitive but effective device.

Wyatt pivoted back toward the barn. He'd overstayed his welcome. "Thank you again for all that you've done. I'll pack up my belongings and wait in my room until someone can take me into town."

"Mr. Darling," Rosemarie paused. "Wyatt, wait."

Wyatt turned a bit too quickly and nearly toppled over. Thankfully, he caught his balance and remained standing. Rosemarie came up beside him. "Are you certain you wish to stay in town?"

He smiled. "Thank you again. You've been most generous and your cooking… A man could do no better. I have the funds now and I shall leave as soon as the doctor says it is safe for me to travel. Being in town will make it easier to arrange transport on a ship heading to Cape Cod."

Rosemarie nodded. "Very well. I bid you good journeys."

"Merci beaucoup, madame."

"De rien." Rosemarie's accent was impeccable.

"I'm afraid we've reached the end of my *français*."

He extended his hand. She placed hers within his. He lifted it with the ease of a gentleman at court, bowed and kissed the top of her hand. "*Adieu ma ami*. Until we meet again. God's blessings on you and your household."

"*Je vous remercie,* M. Darling. God's blessings on you, as well."

Wyatt returned to the barn and began to pack his belongings. The clothes and various items he'd been given since the attack were more than he'd had in many a year. Unfortunately he didn't have a satchel to travel with. He'd returned the one given to him by Mrs. Hutchinson at Dr. Peck's office. A new traveling satchel would be the first item to purchase.

An hour later, his room was packed, the bedsheets stripped and the room ready for the next occupant. He wondered who else might be the receiver of such a wonderful family's hospitality.

"Mr. Darling, Mr. Darling." Amy and Bessie came running in. "Momma said you were leaving. Why?"

The two looked up at him with eyes so captivating it made his heart ache. Tears began to well in his own. He no longer saw just them but the eager anticipation in his own sister's eyes when they left on that fateful trip. He planted a smile and reached out to them for a giant hug. "Come, let me hug you one last time."

The girls snuggled in and embraced him in a gigantic cocoon. He balanced on his good leg and held them tight. "It has been a pleasure to make your acquaintance, dear ones."

"Don't go, stay," Bessie whined.

He reached up and brushed the tender hairs from Bessie's face. "Ah, but little one, it is time. I must return to my home and take care of some much overlooked business." And it was true. If he had purchased his ship, he wouldn't have given Cotuit Port and the family homestead a minute's thought. Instead, he'd been doing nothing but thinking about the past, his responsibilities and such. Wasn't it just like God to remove all the distractions to get one's attention? "You remind me of my own sisters, Deborah and Carol." He kissed the top of each of their heads. He'd grown to love this family as if it were his own.

"Would you girls lend me a hand?" He paused. "I am in need of some twine to bind my bundle of clothing with. Can you fetch me some?"

Amy released him first. "I know where Papa keeps it."

"Wait for me, I wanna help." Bessie trailed behind her sister. Wyatt hopped over to one of his crutches and balanced on one leg. He bent down and picked it up.

"They're a handful, aren't they?" Jack appeared in the doorway. "Mother said you wished to go to town. I'll be happy to take you in the morning." Jack scanned the bed. "On the other hand, I'd be happy to take you now."

"Thank you," Wyatt smiled.

"Give me a minute to pen a note for my wife."

Wyatt nodded his agreement. Jack left and Bessie ran in before Amy. "Amy found the twine," Bessie announced. "Are you in love with Mercy?"

"What?" Mercy stood up and greeted her unwanted guest.

Benjamin ran up to the tent.

Billy held up his hands. "I heard you were salt harvesting and thought it might be as good a time as any to make my intentions known." He wasn't unpleasant on the eyes, with his wavy blond hair and bright blue eyes. He wore the tan of one who spent a fair amount of time working outside.

Benjamin placed his hands on his hips. "A gentleman seeks the father's approval first. Have you spoken with my father?"

"No, I'm sorry. I suppose you're correct. Forgive the intrusion, and most of all, forgive my forward nature, Miss Hastings, Master Hastings." Billy nodded toward Benjamin. "If it be not an imposition, may I have something to drink before I return to town?"

Mercy relaxed her shoulders. "Have a seat, Mr. Crabtree. Sweet tea, lemonade or water?"

"Sweet tea would be wonderful. Thank you, Miss Hastings." Billy surveyed the area.

Only two chairs were set up in the tent. It might be poor manners, but Mercy wasn't inclined to offer up her chair or Benjamin's. Billy sat down on a bundle of firewood. Mercy poured the sweet tea from a pitcher into a tall glass, then handed it to him.

"Thank you, Miss Hastings. You certainly are a sight for sore eyes. I think you're even more pretty now than when we were in school together."

"That's very kind." Mercy's spine stood rigid. Billy had been one of the boys with Robbie who felt she wasn't good enough to be a proper wife. Why this sudden change and why from two of the group of boys? It didn't make sense.

Ben sat down in his chair. "Benjamin, may I pour you a glass, as well?"

"No thank you." Ben turned his focus on Billy. "How'd you know we were out here?"

"I was in the market the other day when Mercy, I

mean, Miss Hastings, was purchasing a new book and some supplies."

Mercy didn't recall having said anything to anyone of their plans. Billy drank a sip of his tea while Mercy sat back down.

"Forgive my inquiry, but is it just the two of you out here?"

"We're expecting others to arrive later."

"Ah." Billy nodded and downed the rest of his tea. "I fear I have gone about this in all the wrong ways. Please forgive my forwardness, Miss Hastings. I shall seek your father's permission and, if he is agreeable, I shall try to win your affections. I am but a humble man, with not much in terms of worldly wealth, but I believe I can provide for a wife and children."

"What of love, Mr. Martin?"

"Ah, yes, love. I believe it is necessary for a good marriage, but it takes time to develop. A wise man will be patient and wait for a noteworthy wife. And you, Miss Hastings are of impeccable character, a hard worker and wise beyond most of your sex. If you would allow me to be so forward."

"This is not how you have always felt."

"No, perhaps not. Many of my gender find it hard to accept a woman who is of strong character. But I have watched and have grown to appreciate your strong will and determination. The recent events of your Samaritan behavior showed a generous and strong heart. I or any man would be a fool not to recognize that."

A gasp escaped her lips.

Billy cocked his head to the right, then looked down at his lap. "I fear you heard of a foolish conversation between myself, Robbie Brown and others. Am I correct in my assessment?"

Benjamin stood.

Billy got down on his knees. "Mercy, forgive me. I was a foolish young man. I am so sorry if my ignorant words hurt you. You are so much more than what we ever thought or dreamed of. Can you forgive me?"

Unable to speak, Mercy didn't respond. Benjamin stepped toward Billy and lent him a hand to get up off the sand. Billy complied and stood. "How can I make it up to you, Mercy?"

Mercy shook her head no. Benjamin escorted him away from the tent.

"What can I do, Ben?"

"Isn't my place to say."

"Of course. Please tell Mercy I'm sorry. She can write me if she changes her mind. I shall not put a request in to your father. It wouldn't be prudent at this time. Good day, Ben."

"Good day, Mr. Crabtree."

Mercy ran over Billy's words. Could they be sincere? And when did Billy start speaking in such tones? She'd never known him to express any proper social graces. He wasn't a rude person, but he wasn't formal in his approach or words. Walking up to them at the beach, that was a Billy approach. But the words that came from his mouth... *Does he really see me as a woman of worth?*

Stunned by Bessie's question, Wyatt hemmed and hawed. How could he answer? He didn't know if he was in love with Mercy or not, but he certainly couldn't entertain the thought, even if he were inclined. "She's a remarkable woman, and I have great affection for her. She saved my life. A man has a special place in his heart for those who save his life."

"So you're not going to kiss and make a baby like Jack and Diane?"

"Bessandra Hastings!" Jack roared. "That is not how a young lady conducts herself. Apologize to Mr. Darling."

"I'm sorry. I don't know what I said wrong, but I'm sorry."

Wyatt found his tongue and smiled. "It's forgotten and you're forgiven."

"You girls go up to the house. Mr. Darling and I will be leaving soon." Jack came into the room and took the bundle of clothes. The girls ran out, toward the house. "I'll bind these for you. My apology for my sister, Mr. Darling. Bessie has always been a bit forward. She's a strong girl, like Mercy, but doesn't seem to be able to control her tongue as well. Of course, that took time with Mercy, too. I remember when we were little, she was four and I was six… Forgive me, I didn't mean to impose my fanciful stories of my sister on you." Jack nodded and left the room. Wyatt penned a quick note of thanks to the Hastingses' household and surveyed the room one last time.

The Lord had met him in this room. Memories of Mercy and her sweet voice playing at his heartstrings caused him pause. He closed his eyes. He couldn't allow himself to go down that path. This was not the time nor the place. Perhaps after he returned to Cotuit Port, he would be able to think more clearly on the matter. For now, moving away from the Hastingses' home and all their temptations was best. He shifted his crutches and walked out the door, closing it behind him.

The ride into town was quiet with the exception of another apology from Jack regarding Bessie's comments. She was nine and too young to understand what she was really asking. Jack unloaded Wyatt's bundles and brought them to the registration desk at the Tropical Breezes Inn. "Be careful, Wyatt." Jack extended his hand.

"Thank you, and thank your family."

"Pleasure. I suppose this is goodbye then. How soon will you set sail for Massachusetts?"

"I am uncertain. I will need to speak with Dr. Peck and find a vessel heading north."

Jack nodded and set his hat back on his head. "Godspeed, Wyatt."

"To you and yours, as well, Jack."

Jack departed, and a middle-aged man with a portly belly and a balding pate stepped behind the counter. "How may I help you, Mr. Darling?"

Wyatt cocked his head. "My apologies, sir. I don't recall having met you."

"Jethro Billings. I've seen you on several occasions driving the wagon for Miss Hastings and Mrs. Martin."

"Pleasure to meet you, Mr. Billings. I've come to rent a room for a week, possibly two."

"I have one on the lower floor. It's a smaller room, but it might be easier than climbing the stairs."

"Thank you. That would be sufficient." Wyatt reached in his pocket and realized he hadn't gone to the bank yet to cash the check.

"Your first week's stay is on me. It was a terrible, terrible mishap you encountered. I told Miss Hastings you had a free week."

Wyatt felt the heat rise on his cheeks. The generosity of strangers seemed to continue. "Thank you."

Jethro rang a small brass bell. A bellhop came in and took his bundles. "Room eleven." The young boy nodded and headed down the hallway to the right. Mr. Billings reached over to a panel of cubbies and pulled out a key. "The wife and I are planning on dinner at six. We'd be honored if you would grace us with your presence this evening."

"Thank you. I look forward to it."

"Great. I'll tell Edith and you can get yourself situated in your room."

Wyatt engaged in pleasantries and headed down the hall. The bellboy came out and held the door open for him to enter. The room was very neat and tidy. It smelled fresh and clean, and it was half the size of the room where he'd spent that last several weeks . He took a few moments unbundling his belongings and placing them in the chest of drawers. First thing in the morning, he would go to the bank, visit with Dr. Peck, then speak with the harbormaster. He placed his Bible by the nightstand, then thought better of it and sat down in a chair under the window. He thumbed through the pages hoping to find some insight into his restlessness. But nothing calmed his desire to be on the sea, heading home…but not really home. His burning desire had nothing to do with Cotuit Port or Captain Nickerson's letter. Instead, it had to do with getting back what had been stolen from him, his own vessel. To be on the sea and free sounded so peaceful right now, not the feelings or desires for Mercy Hastings. He'd done nothing wrong in his relationship with Mercy. Instead, he'd been the perfect gentleman. He didn't take her into his arms and kiss her like he had thought of doing. He could think of nothing else. Instead, he'd been faithful, respectful and still they…they what? What was it exactly they had done?

Wyatt got up to pace. But he couldn't. He eyed the wooden sticks that enabled him to move about and yet he despised having to use them. "Am I so ungrateful, Lord?"

Chapter 10

"What was that about?" Benjamin sat back down. Mercy scanned the road for any other unwanted visitors. Seeing none, she took her seat on the beach. "I realize what he was asking," Ben continued, "but didn't you find it rather peculiar?"

"Yes, and since when did Billy Crabtree start speaking in a proper manner?" Mercy stood up and walked over to the boiling water. Salt was beginning to form on the edges. The process was a long one. Once the salt was boiled down, then they had to add fresh water and dry it again to release the high magnesium content, which is natural in sea salt and makes it bitter. Truthfully, she wondered if there was a need to make salt. She heard that salt was selling for fewer than two dollars a barrel. But her father was the ultimate frugal man. Three days of labor, if he had to pay for it, would cost more than buying several barrels of salt.

Returning to her chair, Mercy shook off the thoughts

about her father and Billy Crabtree and concentrated on the new novel she was reading. The protagonist solving a mystery... Her mind began to wander over the clues the author had given. Would she figure out who did it before the author revealed it to his audience? In her readings, she'd done well solving mysteries. Her mind drifted over to Wyatt and his robbery. What if she could help with the investigation? She sat back down to finish the book and test her investigative skills.

The next morning, she found herself restless. She and Benjamin had taken turns through the night keeping the fires burning, boiling down the salt water and scraping the pot. The first barrel was full. They had started on the second. Today she would start the second pot, reboiling the salt to remove the magnesium. She was tempted to purchase barrels of salt from the merchants with her own money. It wasn't quite the same as when she was younger and the family camped on the beach. Then she was free to play, swim, fish and yes, she worked some, but her parents did most of the labor. No wonder they were excited to have Benjamin and her do the harvest this year.

This morning, she'd seen several people travel north and south on the beach road. Some were walking, some were on horseback and a few drove their wagons. But if she didn't know better, she'd say that Wyatt Darling was traveling in a small buggy. It wasn't one of her father's, so it couldn't be him. She went back to work, ignoring the passersby. Her mind settled on the beating the three men had given Wyatt in order to steal his money belt. First, someone had to have known how much money he had on him. Second, they seemed to want to kill him. They had come close. Why so violent? He wasn't from around here. Who wanted to hurt him?

"Mercy!" Mercy turned toward the tent. Benjamin wasn't calling her. She went back to work getting the pans ready for the refining process.

"Mercy! On the road," the voice called out.

Mercy stopped what she was doing and spun around. "Wyatt?" She ran as quickly as possible in soft sand to the road.

"Forgive me for calling out, but I know I'd never get the sand out of my cast if I were to attempt walking on the beach."

"Nonsense. What are you doing here and where'd you get this buggy?"

"I rented it. I came out to say thank-you for all that you've done in helping me. But I've received word from Cotuit Port and Captain Nickerson sent me some of my money. I'll be traveling home within a week or two. Dr. Peck said I could travel in a week."

A whirlwind of emotions caught Mercy by surprise. She stuffed them down and asked, "Where are you staying?"

"Tropical Breezes Inn. Mr. Billings gave me a small room for the first week."

"He's a good man." She wanted him to stay. She wanted to speak with him. She'd missed him, and it had only been a day. "I'm glad you have good news from Cotuit Port."

He beamed. "Apparently, if you put all your income into savings for fifteen years, you have quite a savings account. I have enough to purchase the boat. I'm on my way to speak with James Earl and see if his steam yacht is still available. I can't purchase it today but perhaps after I return home."

"Will you be able to sail again?"

"I don't know."

"Then perhaps you should not speak with James Earl. Why get the man's hopes up? What use is it to you to purchase a steam yacht if you can't sail it?"

Wyatt's shoulders slumped. "You're right."

Benjamin came out of the tent. "Wyatt, what are you doing here?"

"I came to say thank-you to your sister and you. Mercy will explain. How's the harvesting going?"

Benjamin filled Wyatt in on the progress they'd made so far. Mercy found herself in a strange state of affairs. A part of her wanted to wrap him in her arms and never let him go. Another part of her wanted to strangle him. All he could see was being a sea captain again, nothing else. More important, no one else.

"Excuse me gentlemen, I must get back to work. Wyatt, it was good to see you again. I bid you smooth journeys. Good day." She turned and headed back to the flat pans. Between evaporation and the heat from the fire, they would dry the salt out quickly, and large crystals would form.

Her heart was aching. She'd grown to love Wyatt, and he was so blinded by his own hopes and dreams that he couldn't see how much she cared for him. *Dear Lord, help me.*

Wyatt watched as Mercy headed back toward the beach.

"Wyatt?"

Benjamin… He was speaking with him about something…. "Huh? Forgive me, what were you saying?" Wyatt gave a sideways glance over toward Mercy.

Ben laughed. "You've got it bad."

Wyatt snapped his focus back to Ben. "What?" He could feel the heat rise on the back of his neck.

"I may only be sixteen, but I can see you love my sister."

"I have great affection for her, as I do for your entire family."

"If I caught you looking at me the way you were just looking at Mercy, we might be exchanging fisticuffs."

Wyatt cleared his throat. "I can't afford to fall in love right now. I don't know what my future holds. I planned to be a sea captain and never marry."

"And then you met my sister," Ben supplied.

"Yeah, and then I met your sister. She's a remarkable woman. A man couldn't do better. But I can't offer her a future at this point in time. She's better off with a man who knows he can provide for his family."

"Perhaps. Then again, Father would not allow her to marry a man who didn't have a sound future."

"And that, my friend, is why I moved out. Your parents are concerned that a relationship between Mercy and me will develop. I can't blame them, but I will not put your sister in a compromising position between her love for her parents and her…" Wyatt couldn't finish the sentence.

"Wyatt, let me give you a piece of advice that I recently received from Mercy. Be true to your calling, not what others think you should do."

"You've decided to go to medical school and become a doctor, then?"

"Yes. I don't know how I'll be able to afford it, but I believe it is the right course for me. I understand your wanting to be a sea captain and working so hard for your dream, only to have it taken from you. But is it possible the Lord is using this to make you question the decisions you've made for your life?"

"It's entirely possible. And I have been reevaluating my life and choices. It is one of the reasons I must return to Cotuit Port. I've ignored my responsibilities for far too long."

Ben nodded. "I understand. I shall pray for you, and you can pray for me. I don't believe Father will be opposed to my becoming a medical doctor, but his plans have always been to give the ranch to Jack and me."

"There's always veterinary medicine." Wyatt smiled.

"I'm not that fond of animals. I am intrigued with the mysteries of the body, though. Dr. Peck said he'd allow me to help him with the next dead body and will teach me what the different organs are and how they work."

"Ugh." Wyatt wasn't in the least bit curious how his insides looked or worked. "It takes a certain individual to be curious about such things."

Ben laughed. "I know. I've been examining the animals after they've been killed before they are butchered, and I've been studying the biology books, so I know in drawings how the human body looks...."

Wyatt held up his hand. He didn't consider himself to have a weak stomach, but... "That's enough."

Ben laughed. "You're like most. As you said it takes a certain kind of individual."

Wyatt chuckled. "Yes, and you appear to be one of them. God's blessings on you and your studies."

"Thank you." Ben glanced over to Mercy, then back at Wyatt. "Pray. The Lord will direct your path."

"Thanks, Ben. I know He will. Good day." Wyatt tapped the reins and continued on his way south. Should he turn around as Mercy had suggested and not give James Earl false hope? Deciding she was right, he looped the buggy around and headed north toward town. Taking one long glance at Mercy, he turned his attention back to the road. He caught motion out of the side of his eye and saw her running toward him. He pulled the reins and stopped.

"Mercy?"

"Wyatt," she caught her breath. "Please understand I mean you no ill will. I didn't mean to be harsh with you. Forgive me."

Wyatt leaned toward her. "Nor I you. You are forgiven, Mercy. I could never fault you for anything. You have been such a blessing to me. I…" He stopped before he confessed something he didn't really want to accept.

She reached out and touched the top of his hand. "I shall pray for you, Wyatt."

"And I you, Mercy." He flipped his hand and held hers within his and kissed the top of it. "You are a fair maiden and I am forever in your debt."

Mercy chuckled. "*Vous êtes charmeante,* M. Darling."

Wyatt laughed.

"Parlez-vous français?"

"Un peu."

"Then I shall have to choose my words more carefully." Mercy giggled.

"Mercy, please understand, I do not wish to injure your feelings. I have great affection for you, but…"

She started to pull her hand from his, then caressed it with her own. "I do understand, Wyatt. And I trust God to show you the path you are to walk. I am sorry about the possibility that you may not be able to be captain. I know how hard it is to work for something and, in the end, not achieve it."

Wyatt nodded. His throat was tight. If he gave into his feelings he'd jump down from the buggy and wrap her in his arms. "I shall be in town for a week or two. Perhaps we will have time to see one another again."

"I'd like that. I'd like to hear about this small fortune

you have and hear your plans." A peace settled through him. He had not strained his relationship with Mercy. *Thank You, Lord.*

"There is so much I'd like to tell you, but I need to travel north and take care of my family home."

Mercy nodded. "I understand. Be well, *mon ami*."

"Oui, mon coeur."

Mercy raised her eyebrows. Her blue eyes sparkled. "What? What did I say?"

"You said, 'I will, my heart.'"

"Oh, well…" Wyatt stammered. "You know what I meant."

Mercy smiled. *"Oui, mon ami,* I do." She took her hand from his and stepped away from the buggy. Wyatt slapped the reins perhaps a bit harder than he should have as the buggy leaped forward with a jerk. Perhaps his misspoken French was not wrong. Mercy Hastings held the key to his heart, of that he was certain. He couldn't, and wouldn't, act upon it. But the woman had won his affection.

Mercy spent the next two days working hard on the salt harvest. She had read once that it took three hundred and sixty gallons of seawater to make one bushel of salt, or fifty-six pounds. They would be leaving with two bushel barrels. And yet she couldn't get it out of her mind that if she'd paid four dollars, it would have provided them as much salt. Mercy shook off her thoughts. They were getting her nowhere and it made it difficult to continue harvesting the salt for Father.

Her only distraction had been the mystery novel, but now she had convinced herself to try and figure out who stole Wyatt's money. Where he had been attacked didn't sound like the work of a sailor but rather someone who lived in St. Augustine and knew the roads. They waited until he was out past most of the residences, a place where an ambush could happen without arousing anyone. The three men who attacked Wyatt had to be local, or at the very least, very well acquainted with the area.

"Mercy," Ben called out. "I need your help hoisting the salt barrels into the wagon."

"Coming." Mercy tucked the last of her belongings in her satchel and headed over to her brother at the rear of the wagon. Together, they lifted and strained. "These seem heavier. Probably because Father isn't the one on the other side of the barrel... Sorry."

Benjamin shrugged. "I'm not offended. I haven't developed the muscles that Dad and Jack have. Not yet," he added.

Mercy laughed. "Your day is coming, brother."

"I know. Can't blame me for wanting them."

"Nope. You should have seen Jack around your age. He couldn't stop lifting and curling anything that had some weight to it. It was the only time he volunteered to cut wood."

"Did it work?"

Mercy laughed. "You tell me. Is he a strong man in your opinion?"

"Yeah, I've seen him wrestle more than one steer to the ground. That takes strength."

"Yes it does." Mercy appreciated that her father never encouraged her to take on that part of ranch life. She'd ridden her fair share and camped out many a night, watching cattle, but the branding, roping and all were jobs for the men, and she was grateful.

Benjamin went back to the beach and picked up the last of the remaining bundles, then rolled up tent and stakes. Mercy sat up front and grabbed the reins. She looked off to their left and thought about paying a visit to Earl James to question him about what he knew of the attack. She didn't know him all that well, but did he set up Wyatt? If he truly were moving to Texas with his family, wouldn't he have left the area by now? If he had stolen the money, enough time had passed he could have decided to change his mind and travel with his steam yacht to Texas. But he was still here in St. Augustine. Why wasn't he planning on taking his steam yacht? Wouldn't the travel have been cheaper?

The wagon shifted as Ben climbed up and sat down beside her. "Ready?"

"Yeah. I can't wait to wash off all this salt."

"You and me both. I think I'll jump in the stream and wash the salt off that way."

Mercy nodded. "A good swim would be relaxing."

"Have you decided what you're going to tell Maman and Papa about Billy Crabtree?"

Mercy's stomach flipped, but not in the same way as when she saw Wyatt Darling the other day. "I'm not interested in Billy Crabtree."

"No, you're interested in Wyatt Darling. You can deny it all you want, but you love him." Ben smiled and slid back into a more comfortable position. "Don't worry. I won't say anything to anyone else."

"Especially since Wyatt doesn't feel the same way about me. Maybe he does, but he has his own plans, and they do not include a wife."

"I can understand what Wyatt might be thinking. If I go to school to become a doctor, I won't allow myself to be distracted by a wife. I'll avoid women as much as possible. Avoid is probably not the correct term. But…"

Mercy laughed. "Men. You're all the same. You want

a wife to take care of you, cook your meals, clean your house and all, but there is so much more."

Ben laughed. "Women. You want a man to attach to…. Never mind. You're not the typical woman, and you'd be an asset to any man. I need to stay focused on my goals, first and foremost. Once I have achieved my education, then I'll search for a wife. I would like one, but she has to be the right one."

"Agreed. The right spouse is the best spouse. I shall not settle for less than that myself." Mercy's mind drifted back to Wyatt Darling. He had a handsome face, now that most of the bruising and cuts were healed. His broad shoulders… A flash of Wyatt's scarred back crossed her memory like a bolt of lightning. There were so many things that neither one knew about the other.

She drove the wagon home, checked in with Grace concerning the laundry business, then set her sights on a swim to wash off the salt and sweat from the past three days. She dove into the river and followed the current underwater for a spell. Lost in the peaceful motion, her cares flowed downstream. She surfaced and swam back to the small wooden dock, which held her towels, soap and shampoo. She lathered the shampoo in her hair. Her fingers remembered the gentle touch of Wyatt, his gentle kiss on them. Mercy groaned. "Dear Lord, I need Your help. If he's to be my husband, confirm it for me but also confirm it for him. If not, remove these foolish, fanciful thoughts I've been having."

Mercy dipped back under the water to wash off the shampoo.

"What are foolish, fanciful thoughts?" Amy asked with her hands on her hips.

Mercy sank back under the surface of the water.

Chapter 11

Mercy moved with a graceful manner, and yet her steps were sure and straight. He'd been observing her for three mornings since she'd returned from harvesting the salt. His days had been spent writing letters, making travel arrangements and constant visits with the sheriff. Nothing had come to the surface that brought any light on the men who had beaten him and stolen all his money. But the sheriff had some rather disturbing news this morning, and as much as he wanted to keep his distance from Mercy, he could not hold his tongue on this matter. "Miss Hastings," he called out with a wave. He had positioned himself at a small table at Pedro's. "Would you care to join me for a cup of coffee?"

She smiled. Wyatt reached out and steadied himself. Her lips were a pretty rosebud pink. She lashed the laundry down and walked toward him. His pulse quickened. He closed his eyes and counted to three.

"Good morning, Mr. Darling. It is a pleasure to see you. How is your leg healing?"

"Fine, fine. Can you join me for a cup of coffee?"

She glanced around. "Thank you. I can't stay for long."

Of course not. It was a bold move to ask a woman without a formal invitation. Captain Nickerson had taught him about social etiquette, and he'd even read a few books on the subject, but he wasn't from high society and felt a lot of the rules were rather foolish and a waste of time.

Mercy sat down and bowed her head slightly. Wyatt waved to the waitress, Pedro's wife. "May I have a cup of coffee for Miss Hastings, please?"

"*Sí,* senor." Maria shuffled back inside the café.

"I shouldn't stay for long," Mercy whispered.

"Maria will be our witness." Wyatt winked.

"Wyatt, please don't."

He didn't realize how forward he had been. "I'm so sorry, Mercy. I miss our conversations. I was hoping we could spend some time with one another. I leave in three days."

"Three? I thought you were going to be here for ten."

He reached out to touch her hand and pulled his back before he made contact with her. "It has been five days since I told you that I might have two weeks. Dr. Peck will be changing my cast the day before I leave. That should be the last one until it comes off permanently."

"Is he hopeful you'll be able to walk again?"

"Yes, it is possible. The leg will be weak for quite a while, but if I'm careful it should heal well."

Maria brought Mercy a white porcelain cup. A ribbon of steam spiraled up. "*Gracias,* Maria."

"You're welcome, Mercy." She left them alone.

Wyatt scanned the area and leaned a little closer. "Is

it possible for us to have some time together before I leave? Or am I presuming too much?"

"Come to dinner at my parents' house tonight. We can sit on the porch. Take a walk. We will be able to have a private conversation…relatively private."

"Bessie?"

"The last time, it was actually Amy."

"The last time? There are other gentleman callers?"

"Yes, but that is not what I'm referring to. Amy heard my prayers while I was in the river. I thought I was alone and, well, let us just say that it was an embarrassing moment."

Wyatt nodded. He'd love to know what she was praying that would be embarrassing. But he knew. He had a few of his own that would cause many a head to turn if he weren't careful and prayed aloud. "God hears our prayers even when they are not spoken."

Mercy groaned then laughed. "Trust me, my prayers are *all* private now. I won't be making that mistake again."

"I'd rather…" Wyatt held his tongue. "…not travel down this line of conversation. I thank you for the dinner invitation. I shall be at your house at five, if dinner is still served at that time."

"It's a ranch, Mr. Darling. There is always a schedule, and it always stays the same." Mercy sipped her coffee then stood up. "I shall see you later, Mr. Darling. Have a pleasant day."

"Thank you, Miss Hastings. I shall do my best."

She headed back to the alley at Tropical Breezes and climbed on the wagon. A wheelbarrow was no longer large enough to carry all the wash that she and Grace Martin were doing. He looked down the road and there stood Grace with two bundles of dirty laundry. Mercy stopped the wagon. Grace loaded the soiled linen, and Mercy carried the clean parcels into the small guesthouse at the end of the street. Wyatt marveled at how many visitors came to St. Augustine and at the amount of housing from big hotels to small guesthouses and inns.

Maria came up to the table. "May I bring you anything else, Mr. Darling?"

"*Gracias,* no." Wyatt tapped his stomach. *"Muy bueno."* His Spanish had been increasing while he was staying in town. Wyatt adjusted his crutches and stood up. "Have a good day, Maria."

"And you, Mr. Darling."

Wyatt plopped down a silver dollar. They still would not accept payment for the food he ate, so he made certain to leave a healthy tip every day. In truth, the tip was about the same amount as the meal. He made his way back to the inn and headed to his room.

"Mr. Darling," Jethro Billings called out as he worked his way down the hallway. "There is a telegram here for you."

Mercy helped clean up the dinner dishes as quickly as possible so that she and Wyatt could have a few moments alone. Everyone in the family had engaged him in conversation over dinner. Mercy had watched with utter fascination. The girls loved him. Ben shared with him that he had spoken with his parents and they had agreed to let him pursue an education in medicine. And her parents filled him in on the various events of the past week. The entire family missed him.

Her mother came up beside her. "Go, child. Take him outside and have some time together. But guard your heart, dear."

"I shall." In truth, there was nothing left to guard.

She was in love with Wyatt and content to live the rest of her life as a single person if he never saw her as his spouse. At least, after much prayer, that is what she thought she would do.

"Mr. Darling, would you care to join me on the porch and watch the sunset?"

"I would be honored, Miss Hastings."

Father stiffened. Her mother went over to him and placed a hand on his shoulder. Another example of how strong her mother was in their relationship.

"Can I come?" Bessie asked.

"Bessie, I have a special project for you and Amy," her mother said, and Mercy mouthed thank-you to her mother.

"What?" Amy's voice was filled with eager anticipation.

Mercy held the door open for Wyatt as he skipped along on his crutches. She remembered seeing him on the first day and wondering if he were going to fall down using them. Now they were a part of him. His ease of movement was remarkable. He settled down on the bench swing, which faced the west, a perfect place to watch the sunset.

Mercy joined him and tucked her feet up under herself. "Tell me what is driving you back to Massachusetts?"

Wyatt snickered. "You don't waste time with pleasantries."

"No, I'm afraid I don't."

"I received a letter from Captain Nickerson, and in the letter he challenged me to take full responsibility for my property. He was right. I've been avoiding going home, even thinking about my house and the small farm."

"Why? I mean I realize it is because of the memories. But why did you not even consider selling them before now?"

"I don't believe I'll be selling the property. Even if I return to the sea, I will need a home to return to. One does not spend all his days on the ocean, although it is possible."

"Tell me about your home in Cotuit Port."

Wyatt's body stiffened. He closed his eyes, then opened them and focused on hers. "It's a grand house with two stories and dormers jutting out of the roof, giving the upstairs rooms a window or two each. The downstairs has a front parlor, dining area, kitchen and a less-formal sitting area. There's also a large mud-room for muddy boots, shoes and overcoats. There's a huge wraparound porch across the front and side of the house, perfect for looking over the harbor and cooling off during the summer heat."

"It sounds wonderful."

"It's been in the family for a hundred years. There's another house on the property that's a hundred and fifty years old. It's architecture is more in keeping with New England homes from the seventeen hundreds."

"A hundred and fifty?"

"Yes. There are some homes in the area that go back to twenty years after the pilgrims landed at Plymouth Rock. Most of them are in Sandwich, a town between Plymouth and Cotuit Port."

"I've grown up here. There are some homes that date back, but not that far. The Seminole Indians were more mobile and didn't build houses like we do. And the British burned the city down in 1702, so everything is newer than that." Mercy paused. "I'm sorry. Finish your descriptions and why you feel the need to go back home so quickly."

"As I mentioned, Captain Nickerson wrote, and in the letter, not only did he challenge me to take on my responsibilities but he informed me that he would no longer be able to oversee the caretaker and the properties."

"You mean he's been taking care of things since your parents died?"

Wyatt hung his head and fiddled with his fingers. "Yeah."

"Then you must return. It is your duty."

"Yes." He cupped her hands with his. "It pleases me that you understand my reasons."

"I do understand the need. I am puzzled by the reasons you chose not to take responsibility for your parents' property."

Wyatt winced. She pulled away. "I'm sorry."

"You do have a way of getting to the heart of the matter. The best answer I've come up with is avoidance. I wanted to avoid the painful memories. The fact is, I've been on my own longer than I was a small boy under my parents' care. I wish I could pace right now. That's the hardest part of this broken leg, that I can't pace."

Mercy chuckled. "Stop avoiding the subject and tell me why."

"In truth, I don't know. I'm not going to be overrun with grief, as I would have been when I was a boy. Yet those are the emotions I have when I think about the house and returning to it. They don't make sense, but they are the thoughts and feelings I have. But I shall face it."

Mercy placed a hand on his back. "I shall be in prayer for you. What else is driving you to return now, before your leg is healed?"

"You." The word slipped out before he realized it. "I'm sorry."

Mercy's eyes blazed with the sunset. "There is no need to be sorry. I…" She bowed her head.

He interrupted before she confessed her feelings for him. "Mercy, forgive me for all that has happened between us. It was wrong of me to…"

Mercy jumped up from the bench and walked over to the railing of the porch. Wyatt grabbed his crutches, thought better of it and left them on the deck. She turned. Her eyes glistened. He couldn't entertain any further discussion without his confession of his own feelings for her. "There is another reason I asked to come this evening. Sheriff Bower said he heard you've been asking questions regarding my attack. He is concerned you are trying to investigate on your own."

"You are very good at avoidance. Yes, I have been asking some questions. I believe it has to have been locals. To have attacked where you were…"

"Mercy, stop. Please stop. Whoever these men are, they are dangerous. I can't let you…"

"You can't let me?"

The elevation of her voice caused him to turn and see if others were watching. "Mercy, please."

She stomped back to the bench and plopped back down. "You do not have a say in what I do."

"No but…" He paused. How should he approach her? "They are dangerous men. Think of what they did to me. I would be horrified if something happened to you, my rescuer, my friend."

"Is that all I am? Your rescuer? Are your feelings simply those of gratitude?"

Wyatt groaned. "I'm saying this all wrong. I care for you more than any…" He paused again and rubbed the back of his neck. "Mercy, I am fond of you, you know that, but I decided a long time ago I would not marry. I can't allow my feelings for you to grow. It wouldn't be fair to you."

Mercy relaxed and leaned back. A gentle smile reached the edges of her beautiful pink lips. Wyatt fought back the desire to kiss them.

"If friendship is all that you require, I shall be your friend." She leaned in closer. "However, if you should change your mind, I would not be offended by an offer to court you, Mr. Darling." She winked, and Wyatt's insides twisted. He was back in grammar school, eight years old, and Elsie Michaels had given him a kiss behind the lavender bushes in the schoolyard.

"I pity the man who is to be your husband. He will never be able to say no to you, Miss Hastings."

She mumbled, sat back and crossed her arms over her chest. He couldn't make out the words, and he knew better than to ask. "Promise me you will not pursue your own investigation into my robbery."

"I'll tell the sheriff my suspicions. I make no promises at this point."

Wyatt leaned over and took her hands in his. "Please, Mercy, please don't do this. I could never live with myself if something were to happen to you."

She eased out a pent-up breath and looked into his eyes. Hers glistened. His stomach fluttered. Trying to maintain his composure, he blinked with the speed of a snail. "Mercy," he whispered. "Please."

"For you, Wyatt, I will stop."

He focused on her eyes. She was gorgeous. *Forgive me, Father.* He closed his eyes and cupped her face with his hands. He leaned into her and she leaned into him.

The cowbell rang.

They pulled apart. He released her and focused on the amber sky. The sun had gone down at some point during their conversation.

"Father," Mercy muttered.

Wyatt felt the heat rise on his neck and face. "Perhaps I should leave." Wyatt stood up and balanced himself on his crutches. "May I have the honor of your presence tomorrow? There is a formal dinner at the St. Augustine Hotel tomorrow evening. I would be honored if you would accompany me."

Mercy stood up and patted the top of his right hand. "I would be honored to accompany you. You have not seen me dressed in formal attire."

Wyatt smiled. "No, I have not."

Mercy winked. "Do you have formal attire?"

"I'll manage." He chuckled. He thought of seeing Mercy dressed with the elegance and beauty of her French heritage. His heart beat wildly in his chest.

"What time shall I expect you, Mr. Darling?"

"I shall arrive around six." He nodded because he certainly could not bow. *"Au revoir, mon ami."* He turned to leave.

"Au revoir, mon amour."

He stumbled with his crutches. She giggled. He decided it wouldn't be wise to turn around and face her. Instead, he regained his step and retreated like the evader he was. She knew. He knew. They simply weren't… Wyatt groaned and climbed up on his rented wagon.

Chapter 12

Mercy sat back down on the bench and waited for the rest of the house to retire for the evening. She couldn't face her father, not following his ringing of the cowbell at the moment she and Wyatt would have kissed. The lights dimmed. Mercy silently prayed. *Father, give me the strength to be patient with Wyatt. If he is to be my husband, convince him. I do not want a man who does not know for certain if he wants a wife. I'm trying to understand his convictions, I don't. I...I...*

The door creaked open. "Mercy, may I have a word with you?"

Mercy nodded. Her mother came over in her night-clothes and robe. "It's a beautiful evening."

The weather was the least of her concerns.

"I do not wish to pry." Mother sat down beside her. "But if you wish to talk about your feelings and desires, I will listen."

"Oh, Momma." Mercy leaned into her mother's embrace. "I love him. I know you and Father don't approve."

"Shh, it is not that we don't approve, *ma chérie*. We were concerned about the age difference. And Mr. Darling made it quite clear that he was planning a life at sea without a wife and family."

"I know. And if I could have prevented myself from falling in love with him, I would have." Mercy paused. "I mean… Oh, I don't know what I mean. I didn't plan on falling in love with him. And there is so much I do not know about him yet. But I am praying that if he is to be my husband that he will have no doubt."

Mercy pulled away and wiped the tears from her eyes. "He has asked me to attend a formal dinner tomorrow evening. He is attracted to me, but he has not seen me all dressed up."

Rosemarie chuckled. "Then he will be shocked."

"Oui. Je cache ma beauté."

"Yes, you've kept your beauty well hidden, except for the occasional ball or social affair. The men are quite taken aback to discover you're the same woman they see working laundry. Don't you think you should have asked for permission to attend dinner with Mr. Darling?"

"Perhaps but…"

Her mother raised a hand. "It is all right. Your father and I heard him ask, and your father and I trust you."

Mercy sat back and relaxed. "I'll wear the newest dress from the English design, without the bustle."

"The bustle is still quite popular, dear."

"I know, but you know me. I never cared for those things and wore the smallest one possible."

Rosemarie giggled. "I know. I didn't care for them, either, and such a waste of fabric. In one dress, there's enough material to make another. You'll be wearing the lavender dress with the white ruffled bottom and the special beading you put on the bodice?"

"Yes. I'll fix my hair with a string of small pearls braided throughout. And I'll wear *Grand's* silver-and-pearl hair comb."

"Finished off with your hanging pearl earrings and the silver necklace with a black-and-white pearl pendant, *oui?*"

"Oui."

"You are right, Mr. Darling will be in shock. You'll knock him off his crutches. However, we should discuss one more point."

Mercy paused and looked down at her lap. She clasped her hands and sighed. "When Father rang the bell?"

"Yes."

"Is it wrong to want to kiss him?" Mercy asked but didn't wait for a response. "It was probably for the best that Father rang that bell."

"And what is this Wyatt said about you investigating?"

Mercy groaned. "Don't you see? It had to be someone from St. Augustine to know the right place in the road to attack him and be safe from being seen."

"Perhaps so, but isn't that Sheriff Bower's job?"

"But why hasn't he found out who was behind this?"

"Because the ones who stole the money and beat Wyatt must be hiding their guilt well. They must not have spent the money. Or if they are spending it, they are doing so without raising suspicion. You will not pursue questioning people about this matter?"

"No. I gave Wyatt my word."

"Good. Your father would not let you out of the

house if you decided to continue on your own. Whom did you speak with?"

"James Earl, the man selling the boat to him, the banker and a few others. No one remembers anyone noticing he had that much money on him, but someone had to."

"Or they were simple thieves and didn't realize how much Mr. Darling had on him at the time."

"Perhaps. It is peculiar."

"Yes. But it is not your place to be a detective." Her mother pulled the novel Mercy had been reading at the beach out of her house-robe pocket. "Is this why you felt the need to investigate?"

Mercy nodded.

"This is fiction. One cannot assume they know enough by reading a novel. Remember, Emile Gaboriau writes a fanciful tale that keeps one turning a page. He is in control of the story. You, *ma chérie,* are not. God is the author of our lives and the events that happen to us in a day. Are you more knowledgeable than Him?"

"No." Mercy turned away from her mother and concentrated on her lap.

"No, and neither am I. Even Mr. Darling has been learning that lesson with regard to this robbery. You must, too. The sheriff is a good man, an honest man. Let him do his job. And Mr. Darling is correct—these are dangerous men. It is best to not pursue this matter any further."

Mercy nodded.

Rosemarie tapped her daughter's knee and stood up. "I must go to bed. Morning comes early. You should consider doing the same."

"I shall." Mercy lifted her gaze. *"Merci beaucoup, ma maman. Bonne nuit."*

"Bonne nuit." Rosemarie leaned over and kissed the top of her daughter's head. "With regard to Mr. Darling, keep praying. The Lord will direct the two of you."

Mercy watched her mother slip back into the house. She gazed at the starlit skies. "Father, forgive me for pursuing those who robbed and beat Wyatt. Bring them to justice, Lord. And give Wyatt a peaceful night. Help us understand Your will for us."

The snap of a twig drew Mercy's attention. She paused. Her heartbeat pulsed with greater intensity.

Wyatt polished his boot. Tonight would be his last night with Mercy. He'd almost cancelled and thought better of it. He was drawn to her like no other. But he would not give in to his desires. It was best for her to find a husband who would be home every night. And he knew if he had a wife at home, he'd be less inclined to take on some of the more profitable cargo runs from South America to New York. If he were to have a wife, he'd want her with him, night and day. His mind drifted to the thought of Mercy sharing the captain's quarters on his own ship. He shook his head and polished his boot with greater fervor.

Sailors wouldn't sail with him if he had a woman on board. Omens and fables coursed through sailor's veins as easily as one breathed. Admittedly, he had his own fair share, and a woman being on board, even a woman who was his wife, well… There weren't many tales of good adventures with spouses on board. He flexed his back. The scars buoyed his resolve. But then there was Eleanor Cressy, navigator for the *Flying Cloud* alongside her captain-husband, Josiah. He shook off the mind-spinning thoughts and concentrated on the evening before him.

Tonight would be special. They would enjoy themselves and ignore his past. But he could not allow himself to believe or hope for more. The memories they created tonight would have to last him a lifetime.

He slipped his foot into the new black-leather dress boot. The right one would stay in the room. The tailor had opened the seam on the right leg of his trousers rather than cutting the pant leg off, easily mendable in the future. He stood at the mirror, clean-shaven, in top hat and tails. He adjusted his tie, making certain it was centered, then put in the tiepin, holding it in place. He gently eased out a pent-up breath. There was a noticeable change in his appearance, with the hook in his nose from the break it had suffered during his attack.... He turned his head toward the right, then back to the left. It wasn't too bad. Perhaps it even made him look more rugged.

He hobbled over to the door and exited his room. Tonight would be a good night.

The drive out to the ranch seemed to take forever. Amy and Bessie greeted him on the back porch. They were all giddy and bouncy. Benjamin sat on the porch swing and eyed him carefully. But that was nothing compared to the scrutiny he received from Jackson Hastings. "Good evening, sir."

"Good evening. Are you a man of honor?" Jackson asked with a glint in his eye.

"Yes, sir."

"Good. Remember that while you escort my daughter this evening."

"Yes, sir."

Rosemarie came down the stairs. "She'll be down in a moment. You look debonair tonight in your top hat and tails, Mr. Darling."

"Thank you, and you're as beautiful as always, Mrs. Hastings."

His eyes turned to the creak on the stairs. His heart stopped. He forgot to breathe. Mercy stood in all the radiant beauty he'd never beheld in her before. She was stunning, shapely and wonderfully made. "Mercy, you are dazzling."

She smiled. His heart hammered in his chest. He'd known her to be beautiful, but she was elegance and grace all rolled up into one. She would be the queen at any ball, dance or social occasion. "You're so beautiful. You take my breath away." His eyes widened. "Pardon me, I didn't mean to speak so forthrightly." She was dressed in lavender and pearls. The white ruffled skirt under the lavender one peaked out as she descended the stairs.

Jackson Hastings came up beside him. "You see why I so carefully protect her."

"Yes, sir. I shall protect her, as well."

"Good. You have my blessings." Jackson stepped back and put his arm around Rosemarie.

"Good evening, Mr. Darling. You're rather fetching yourself. One might even say ruggedly handsome." Mercy giggled.

Wyatt joined in the gaiety. "I wish I could give you my elbow and escort you the way a gentleman properly escorts a lady, but you must forgive my four legs, because I am still in need of the two extra ones."

"We'll manage."

Benjamin held the door open, and Mercy stayed half a step behind Wyatt and let him lead the way.

He ushered them to the wagon and assisted her as she climbed on board his buggy. Scanning the humble vehicle, he wished he'd rented a fancy carriage for the evening. He hobbled over to the other side and climbed in. Mercy had all the moves of a refined lady. He couldn't believe she was the same woman who hauled soiled linens, worked hard and… But it was her and she was glowing.

"You take my breath away, *ma coeur*."

"So, you do know what that means."

He jiggled the reins and the wagon gently edged forward. "Yes. It slipped out the first time, but I am using it correctly and with purpose tonight."

"Then you do love me."

He turned his gaze back toward her and not the road, giving the horse his head. "Oh, Mercy, how can you think otherwise? Yes, but I…" He refocused on the road. "Let's not spoil this evening. Tonight we are two young lovers enjoying each other and enjoying the evening. It is our last one together."

Mercy bowed her head. He glanced back at her. "I shall try. I don't want this to be our last night together. But if you insist then I will try to understand."

"Thank you. It is the way it has to be. I do love you, Mercy. More than I ever hoped I would be able to love anyone. And there is a huge part of me that doesn't want to leave. But I must. It is my duty."

She reached over and placed her hand upon his forearm. "I know, my love. I know you must, and I want you to go to Cotuit Port and deal with what you've been running away from for so long. It is your family home. It is your inheritance."

Wyatt nodded. "Thank you. It makes it easier, knowing you are supporting me in my decisions."

"Some of your decisions. I support your going back to Cotuit Port. I do want you to question your desires to remain single. I want you to think and pray about the possibility that maybe the Lord has other plans for you. Ones that could include me in your future."

"You have no idea how much I want that to be true. But I learned the hard way there are certain rules one should not break while at sea."

"Such as?"

"Women should not be allowed to travel on board ships as part of the crew. Taking a female passenger from place to place is all right, but the wife of the captain… Well, let's just say I learned the hard way."

Mercy narrowed her gaze. "Wyatt, would you trust me with this knowledge of your past? What happened? I fear it was something dreadful."

Wyatt took in a deep breath and released it slowly. They swayed with the gentle rocking of the buggy. "When I was traveling in the Far East I was on a ship where the captain took his bride. At first, everything was all right. But then the murmurs began. Some of the crew talked about the curse of having a woman on board. Then the winds died down. We were sitting for days without the slightest breeze. Then finally the winds began to pick up and we were sailing again. We were less than a day out from port when pirates raided us. Half of the crew joined the pirates. The captain and his bride were killed, along with the first mate. The pirates believed there was gold on board. I wouldn't give up the location of the gold, which I couldn't because there wasn't any. And I wouldn't join them, so they keel-hauled me before they left me and several other crew members off on a small island."

"Is that how you got those scars on your back?"

"You saw…I remember… The first day, you must have seen them then."

"Yes."

"So you see, if I were to marry you, I would want you by my side on as many voyages as possible. But there is the men's belief in a curse. I vowed then I would not take a wife."

"Ah, I understand."

"Thank you. I couldn't put you in danger."

Mercy smiled.

"What? What am I missing?"

"Nothing. I simply know how to pray now."

Wyatt groaned. "All right, love. For tonight, we are lovers and nothing will stand in our way. Not the future, vows made in the past, the past, nothing. Tonight, it is simply you and me."

"I like that. And Wyatt, if you never change your mind, I will be content. But I must warn you, God is quite capable of changing our minds."

"Yes, He is. And I promise I will pray."

"Thank you. That is all I ask." She leaned over and kissed him on the cheek. He dropped the reins and cupped her face. "I'd kiss you now but we'd mess up your hair."

"Perhaps later." She winked.

Wyatt's insides tumbled like a gale-force wind. He was sunk and he knew it. He reached down and picked up the reins. "You're an incredible woman, Mercy Hastings. You were my rescuer and now, well, now, you're intoxicating and I'm having a difficult time thinking straight."

Mercy giggled. "We shall have a grand evening, Wyatt."

Wyatt chuckled. "Yes, we will." They arrived at the entrance and a porter helped them out of their buggy and took it to a parking area, giving Wyatt a ticket stub to recall his buggy when it was time to leave. Two men opened both doors for them to proceed through. Wyatt hopped forward and, half a step behind him, Mercy reached for the back of his elbow. "You honor me, Mercy."

"*Oui,* it is my honor to be with the most ruggedly handsome man tonight."

"I'm sorry I cannot dance with you."

"That is all right. Maybe the next time." Mercy winked.

Wyatt groaned, then chuckled. The headwaiter took them to their seats. The band played quietly in the background. Images of Mercy being at his side the rest of his life filled him with joy. *Tonight I'll let my imagination run wild. Tomorrow comes soon enough.*

With the devotion of a young lover, he gazed on Mercy. She was incredible. Her beauty captivated him. She inspired him.

She caught his gaze. "What?"

"You. You are incredible. I can't believe I've been blessed to have met you, to know you..." He leaned in closer and whispered, "...to love you."

"And I you, *mon capitaine.* Let us take this fantasy further. Let us pretend we are engaged to marry."

"You are presumptuous."

"*Oui,* but I know *votre coeur.*"

"Something...heart?"

"Your heart." The waiter came and poured water for each of them and took their orders. "So, what is this a benefit for?"

They worked their way through the meal, teasing one another, loving one another and enjoying each other's presence. Then Sheriff Bower came over. "I trust Mr. Darling has spoken with you, Miss Hastings."

"Yes, sir. I won't interfere with your investigation any further."

"Good. These are dangerous men."

"You know who they are?"

"I'm narrowing down the possible options, yes. Trust me, Miss Hastings, I am investigating to the fullest."

Mercy hung her head.

"Sheriff Bower, Miss Darling meant no disrespect." Wyatt defended her.

"No, I imagine she did not. Did you impress upon her the violent nature of these thieves, which she saw full evidence of?"

"Yes, sir. And she has given me her word."

Sheriff Bower turned back toward Mercy. "You are fetching this evening, Miss Hastings. I understand your desire to help Mr. Darling but…"

Mercy held up her hand. "Yes, sir. You've made your opinion quite clear. I shall not investigate further. But you do realize they had to be locals."

"No, I do not. It is probable but not without the possibility that a shipmate might have had it out for Mr. Darling. He is said to have been a fair leader. However, there are those who would not sail with him again."

Mercy glanced over at Wyatt. Wyatt nodded.

"Good evening, Miss Hastings, Mr. Darling."

Wyatt sipped his coffee and turned to his dessert. "Finish, and we will escape before the speeches begin."

"Where shall we go?"

Wyatt smiled and winked. "It is our fantasy night. How about a late-night ride in the moonlight?"

"Sounds wonderful. And improper."

"Ah, well, a slow ride back to your ranch, and we can spend a few moments on the back porch."

"That would be acceptable."

Wyatt would like to take this fantasy a bit further but he'd promised her father he was an upright man, and he knew he would not do anything to dishonor Mercy. Their buggy arrived just as someone called out, "Mercy Hastings is that you?"

Chapter 13

Mercy turned and found Billy Crabtree, Robbie Brown and Michael Shaw. "I see you are already being courted. You could have told me," Billy sneered.

Robbie's face contorted with disgust.

"Forgive us, gentleman, but our buggy has arrived." Wyatt led her to their carriage.

"That woman is not the prim and proper lady you see before you tonight," Robbie droned.

Once Mercy was settled in the buggy, Wyatt turned toward the men. "I do not know you gentlemen. Where I come from, a man does not speak ill of a lady. You, sirs, are beyond contempt."

"You want her, you can have her. Word is she's been alone with you in many compromising positions."

"Excuse me." Wyatt leaned toward the men.

"Wyatt, please," Mercy called out.

Wyatt narrowed his gaze on Robbie Brown. "You,

sir, are no more than a slimy sea slug. If my leg was not injured…"

Robbie charged toward him. Wyatt deflected him and hit him hard against his back with his crutch. "Do not be fooled, Mr. Brown. I can take you and your friends."

Robbie pushed himself up off the street. A crowd had gathered. Robbie stood up and scanned the crowd. Sheriff Bower edged his way to the center. "What's all the commotion?"

"These men—" Mercy cut off her words.

The sheriff took an immediate assessment. "Mr. Darling, may I suggest you take Miss Hastings home. Billy, Robbie and Michael, you've been drinking. Go on home before you get yourselves in trouble."

Wyatt hobbled over to the buggy and climbed up. Robbie and the others scurried off in the opposite direction. "Good night, Mr. Darling, Miss Hastings."

Wyatt tipped his top hat and grabbed the reins. Neither of them spoke for several minutes, then Wyatt began. "I'm sorry, Mercy. I'm afraid I've ruined your honor."

Mercy chuckled. "No, you haven't. Those three have not liked me since we were in grade school together. Now you see why I wasn't interested in pursuing a relationship with either Robbie or Billy."

"Billy? He approached you?"

"Yes, while Benjamin and I were harvesting the salt. He was far more genteel than Robbie, but…" She let her words trail off. He didn't need to know about the past, not yet.

"Was Billy one of the boys who spoke inappropriately about you when you were in school?"

"You know about that?"

"Your father told me."

"Yes, he was." She turned and faced him. "Don't you find it odd they would approach me after saying such hurtful words? And it appears they still believe them, judging from what Robbie spewed out this evening."

"Yes, and you and I both know we have been honorable in our behavior with one another."

Mercy slipped closer toward Wyatt. He put the reins in his left hand and wrapped her in his right. "I'm so sorry, love. You are far more precious than either of those men could possibly see. I am honored by your love and friendship."

She wanted to plead with him to allow himself to marry her but knew only God could make that change. Instead, she snuggled closer and laid her head on his shoulder. "I love you, too, Wyatt."

He kissed the top of her head. Joy infused her body. She could wait for him. She only needed to pray and be patient.

"So, tell me, how many of these social functions have you attended? You have all the poise and grace of a refined proper lady."

"More than I care to admit. Father is often invited, and then there was my coming-out ball, which was a waste of time, since none of the boys wanted to pursue a relationship with someone as bold and direct as me."

Wyatt laughed. "They were stupid boys."

They spent the rest of the evening, on into the late hours of the night, talking back at the ranch. Finally, he kissed the top of her hand and departed. She did not see him the next day, although she tried. She went to the port but missed his ship by minutes. The ship was gently easing out into the harbor as she arrived. She waited for a glimpse of him on the deck and was not disappointed when she saw him standing on his crutches. He lifted his left arm and waved. She waved back. *"À bientôt!"* she called.

"Au revoir!" He replied. And even though she knew he understood her salutation, she understood his. He believed it was the last time they would see one another. She, on the other hand, was more and more convinced that the Lord would change his mind, and one day he would return. *Oh, Father, protect him and work Your healing upon his heart. I understand his fears but I believe You are more powerful and can restore him.*

Wyatt watched as Mercy became a small dot on the shore. He closed his eyes and remembered the feel of her in his arms the night before and the joy in their conversations with one another. *Father, give her peace.*

The ship's captain was a friend, and he agreed to drop Wyatt off in Cotuit Port. It felt good to feel the gentle rhythm of the waves under his feet. He was indeed less stable on the crutches, but even so, he maneuvered well on deck. The voyage would take five days because of the various stops along the way. Wyatt found himself thinking of Mercy more and more with each passing day.

He sat down in his quarters and began to write her a letter.

Mon Coeur,
It is with deep regret I left you in St. Augustine. I know in my heart it was the right thing to do. I miss you and will continue to write to you. I do not know whether I shall send these letters. I do not wish you more pain. But I am doing as you requested and I am praying for the Lord to direct my

path. For the first time since my family perished I
am actually excited to go and see the house. As I
mentioned before, it is a grand house, one that has
much character and charm. I know that you would
enjoy seeing it. I do not know if you have ever traveled to the North and have seen the architecture.
It is quite different from the homes in your area...

Wyatt finished the letter, folded it and sealed it with
wax. On the outside, he wrote her name and address.
This was the first of many letters he composed over the
next couple of months.

Cotuit Port no longer held bitterness. Instead, he
found peace walking the farm. The house would need
new tenants. Wyatt walked into his parents' bedroom.
The room was the same, but the wallpaper had changed.
The paint on the baseboard and door frames was different. The hardwood floor was covered with a braided
rug. The furniture was in storage in the barn as tenants had used their own belongings. Wyatt gave the
now-empty room one more scan. He could see Mercy
standing in the bay window looking out on the harbor.

He glanced back at the empty window. What did
he want? A wife to strengthen him and his days? Or
to be alone looking out the window without anyone?
And who would continue the family legacy if he didn't
marry and have children? The delicate shape of Mercy
returned. He could imagine her sitting in the bay window. This time, she was rubbing her protruding belly.
A child, their child. Wyatt eased out a pent-up breath.

He knew now that God was the One encouraging
them to be husband and wife. He was walking with a
cane, and all indications were good that he could re-

turn to the sea. He would set sail for St. Augustine in the morning.

The next morning he procured his mother's jewelry box from the barn, he found his grandmother's pink-diamond wedding ring. He slipped it in his pocket. Mercy said she believed in him, that she believed they were to be husband and wife. "Father, thank You for showing me I was not trusting You but fearful because of the past."

A wooden knock bounced off the barn door. "You'll return in the spring, Mr. Darling?"

"Yes, sir. If you find someone in need of the place for the winter, by all means rent it out. But I aim to bring my bride home in the spring."

"A bride is a mighty fine thing, Mr. Darling. My Martha and I, we've been married for going on thirty years. I would be a poorer man without her."

"I'm beginning to understand that now. Mr. Smith, again, I want to thank you for all the fine work you've done on the place. You worked well with Captain Nickerson and oversaw my needs...."

The older man rested one of his beefy hands on Wyatt's shoulder. "Son, what happened to your family was tragic, and you being all alone at thirteen, well, it's a hard life lesson to grow through. You've been in our prayers, and we've been blessed taking care of your farm. It's given me and my family good income for many years."

"And many more years to come. I want to be clear on that. I might be returning, but I'm still going out to sea. I will need you to help run this place."

"It will be my pleasure."

"Please set out two barrels of apples and one of pears for me to take south."

"I'll have them at the dock within the hour."

"Thank you." Wyatt extended his hand.

Jason Smith took the proffered hand and squeezed it firmly. "I'll have the furniture in the house before you return. Just remember to send a telegram before you leave port."

Wyatt chuckled. "I will." Wyatt remembered the shocked stares he received when he'd arrived unannounced. He hoisted a small bag for traveling on his shoulder and proceeded to walk toward the harbor with his leg in a cast but only a cane to aid him. He'd been walking on his leg for three weeks now. By the time he arrived in St. Augustine, the final cast would be ready to be taken off.

He turned and glanced back at the old house. It stood proudly and spoke of five generations of Darlings. With God's blessings he and Mercy would start the sixth.

Mercy finished her chores. She'd been giving more and more of her business over to Grace Martin. Mercy was now living in Wyatt's room in the barn. Her mind drifted back to when Wyatt's presence seemed to overtake the entire room. She sat in the chair and held the couple of letters she'd received from him over the past couple months. Not one word of his feelings for her or a possible future together, but there was a lifting of the burden he seemed to be carrying the entire time he was in St. Augustine.

Thinking back on their final night together brought a smile to her lips as she caressed the folded edge of the envelope. The evening had not been completely ruined by Robbie Brown and Billy Crabtree. She now knew Robbie's only reason for trying to court her was because his father was cutting him off. His lack of a strong work ethic had prompted his father to take drastic measures. Robbie never did like to work hard. Instead, he seemed to be drinking more.

School resumed a couple weeks ago, and Benjamin's teacher had structured his courses to meet his medical-education needs. Father had agreed to pay his entire education, much to everyone's surprise. He also agreed that harvesting their own salt was no longer frugal, given the current prices.

Mercy went back outside to her laundry and started to fold the towels.

"A penny for your thoughts." Her mother dried her hands on her apron and sat down beside her.

"They're all over the place. I'm excited for Benjamin but concerned that I haven't heard from Wyatt."

"I thought as much. Do you still believe he is the one God has planned for you to spend the rest of your life with?"

"Yes, but I'm content if he doesn't choose marriage."

"Are you?"

"I'm trying to be. Momma, I do love him. I understand his fears. What happened with his family, how he received those awful scars on his back…"

"He told you how that happened?"

"Yes, it was as you suspected. He was keelhauled." Mercy filled in the details of the mutiny and how that had cinched his decision not to marry.

"Gracious, that must have been horrible. God will work it out, *ma chérie*. Why are you giving so much of your business to Grace?"

"She needs the income more than I do."

"You are generous to a fault, *ma chérie*."

"Perhaps. But Grace… Well, you know about Grace and her situation with her parents. I've been blessed with parents who allow me to make mistakes but protect me when I need protecting."

"It is hard to let your children go. You want to protect them and keep them safe, even when they are adults making their own decisions. Benjamin is very excited about the festivities this evening."

Mercy gave a halfhearted smile. The last time she dressed up was for Wyatt and their final evening together. "It will be a grand festival."

"He's content to be your escort. And after the confrontation at the… Well, you know your father believes it safer that either he or your brother accompany you. Did I mention your father and I also received an invitation to attend tonight?"

"Are you attending?"

"No. JoJo ate something that made him colicky. Your father will be up half the night, making certain JoJo is all right."

"You can come with Benjamin and me."

"My place is with your father. Helping him with the livestock is part of being a rancher's wife."

Mercy knew all too well the endless number of nights her parents had stayed up caring for their animals.

Ben came running into the room. "Mercy," he huffed. "I've got a telegram for you."

"What is it?"

"Wyatt is returning to purchase James Earl's steam yacht. He's hoping to visit while he's in the area."

Mercy bolted up. "When will he be arriving?"

Ben scanned the message. "It doesn't say." He handed the telegram to Mercy. "Dear Miss Hastings, I am returning to purchase the steam yacht. I would be honored to visit with you and your family, *Ma couer*."

"Ma couer" said it all. She was about to scream with

excitement but thought better of it. "Thank you, Ben." She handed the telegram to her mother. "Mother said you were excited about attending the party tonight."

"Yes, very. I had to order a new suit. I've outgrown my other one."

The party tonight was simply a celebration for the summer's passing before the winter months set in. Winter was her favorite season. Rarely did it get too cold. The Florida heat was far more of a problem.

Mother read the telegram and smiled. She, too, understood the meaning of the last two words. Joy flooded Mercy's soul. The problem would be getting through the next week while waiting for his return.

"I say it's time to leave. The sheriff is getting too close." Billy sipped his beer.

"Nope. I heard Wyatt Darling is returning to purchase James Earl's boat, which means he'll be coming with additional cash. I say we wait and double our take." Robbie chugged down the rest of his beer and wiped his mouth with his sleeve.

"I think we have enough. Let's go." Michael pushed his beer aside.

"Nope, it's my idea, and we're going with it."

Michael leaned back in the booth. Billy leaned forward. "Agreed," Billy said.

"Good. Here's the plan…"

Chapter 14

Wyatt clutched the rail as the ship banked to the starboard side and turned into St. Augustine harbor. His heart pounded. He took in a deep pull of air and eased it out slowly. From the moment he let his heart settle on marrying Mercy, his mind had been flooded with possible images for their future. He could see himself taking her on board as he worked up and down the East Coast. He could see them building a family in Cotuit Port.

His money belt was filled with newspaper cut to the size of bills. It wrapped his hips. He would not make the same mistake twice. James Earl would have to meet him at the bank and receive his money there. He would bring the bill of sale. He didn't believe James Earl was behind the robbery, but he would not repeat a foolish mistake like that. He had wired Sheriff Bower of his arrival from Port Royal, South Carolina, their last stop. If the men who robbed him before were still in the area, they might find him an easy target today. He hadn't informed Mercy for that very reason. He didn't want her caught in the crosshairs. On the other hand, he couldn't wait to see her.

He tapped his grandmother's ring in his pocket. He wore a fashionable suit of the latest English style. His left boot was new. The right boot was in his baggage along with the bank note to transfer his funds to James Earl. A visit with Dr. Peck was the first order of business, then on to the Hastings ranch. With any luck, he'd be walking up to their place without a cast on his leg.

Sailors hustled down the deck, taking down the sails, binding them to the yardarms and preparing the ship to be docked. The first mate called out orders and all obeyed. A peace washed over Wyatt as he watched the familiar sight. He glanced at the dock. *Was he hoping to see Mercy, even though he hadn't given her a specific time or date?* Wyatt chuckled at the absurdity of it all.

But lo and behold, there she stood on the dock, waving. His heart soared. He waved back. Of course she would figure it out. He marveled at the wisdom God graced her with. She would definitely keep him on his toes. The minutes ticked away at such a slow pace, he would have jumped overboard if he knew how to swim. The ropes cinched, the gangplank raised, Wyatt grabbed his bag and headed toward her.

"*Mon coeur,* it is so good to see you."

"*Mon amour,* it is good to see you."

"The sun is setting. You should not be on the docks." He pulled her into his embrace.

"I couldn't help myself."

"It is good—"

"Hand it over." A masked man with a pistol pulled on the two of them jumped out of the shadows.

Wyatt pushed Mercy behind him. "Hand what over?"

"Don't play coy with me," he said in a raspy voice, trying to disguise it. But Wyatt recognized the voice and he knew Mercy did, as well. "Hand it over, now!"

Wyatt lowered his right hand and removed his money belt. The man pushed Wyatt into the harbor and ran away. Wyatt flailed his arms and legs. He didn't know how to swim, never took the time to learn.

Without thought, Mercy dove in. She reached her arm across his chest. He stopped flailing and rested in the confidence of her abilities. She swam him over to the ladder. "You're going to have to teach me how to swim."

Mercy laughed. "I can't believe a sailor like you never learned."

"Most sailors don't."

"That's foolish," Mercy said as Wyatt climbed the ladder with ease, even with a soggy cast. Within moments, a group of men gathered around and helped him up on the dock, besides helping Mercy.

"I was planning on seeing Dr. Peck to have my cast removed. Now I have no choice." He turned and faced the men. "Did the sheriff catch them?"

Sheriff Bower stepped forward. "Yes. I reckon you recognized the one who held you up this time."

"Yes, sir. It was…"

"…Robbie Brown," Mercy supplied.

"Yes, and he, along with Billy Crabtree and Michael Shaw, were the ones to attack you the first time. Michael came forward a couple days ago. His conscience got the best of him. He told me where the other funds were kept, and I'll be retrieving them within the hour. Once the money is accounted for, I'll return it to you, Mr. Darling."

"Thank you, sheriff. I'm glad our plan worked." He turned and saw Mercy shivering. "If you'll excuse us. We need to get out of these wet clothes."

"Come to my office in the morning, and we'll sort out the various charges, hearing dates, etcetera."

"Will do."

Once the sheriff was out of earshot, Mercy turned to Wyatt. "You set this up?"

"You were not supposed to be here. There was a reason I didn't tell you the exact day I was returning." He winked.

Mercy wrapped her arms around him, and he leaned down, lifted her chin and pressed his lips ever so tenderly upon hers. Mercy's heart soared. They were linked, one heart, one body, one soul. She could feel it in her bones. She prayed he felt it, too.

He bent down on one knee. "Mercy, I am a foolish man. I only wish you will continue to see beyond that and continue to love me, as I love you, with all my heart and affection. Please join me as my wife and sail the high seas, live on our family land and bless me with more than I deserve. You are my love, my life. Will you be my wife?"

Mercy took his hand and pulled him to stand beside her. "You know I will. I love you, Mr. Darling."

"And I love you, my good Samaritan and so much more."

They clutched one another and kissed with all the longing that had been buried for so long. They pulled apart as their senses cleared and they remembered where they were. Wyatt grasped her hand and led her to Dr. Pike's office to remove the soggy cast from his leg. Mercy followed and hoped she could borrow a dry dress from one of Dr. Peck's sisters. As they walked, Wyatt passed on all his dreams for their future.

Mercy chuckled. "Don't I get a say in all of this?"

Wyatt roared with laughter. "But of course, *mon coeur,* I wouldn't expect anything less."

"I agree with all your plans, except one."

Wyatt paused. "Which one?"

"The date of the wedding. It shall not be in the spring. It will be as soon as we can put a proper one together. I'm thinking October might be nice."

"That's only a few weeks away."

"I'm not a fancy lady. I like the finer things, but I don't need an elaborate ceremony. I simply want to marry you, be your wife and, well, we'll figure out the rest." Mercy chuckled.

Wyatt swept her in his arms and lifted her off the ground. Mercy squealed. "Mrs. Darling, you are going to keep me on my toes."

"As often as possible."

Epilogue

Mercy sat at the bay window, scanning the Cotuit Port Harbor, rubbing the baby within. The house was all that Wyatt had promised and so much more. She loved the cooler temperatures. The water was deeper blue and colder. With these temps she understood why Wyatt had never learned to swim, even as a boy. He knew how to swim now, and so would this little one. She smiled.

"Mercy," Wyatt came running in and stopped short just as he entered their bedroom. "Oh, *mon coeur*." His voice was unsteady.

"What's the matter?"

"Nothing. I was walking around the house shortly after deciding to ask you to marry me, when I had a vision of you sitting in front of that very window, expecting our child. I guess I never imagined I would see it for real one day. God has blessed me far more than I deserve."

"Blessed us. Come here, handsome, and give me some love."

Wyatt smiled and leaped forward, lifting her into his arms. *"Mon coeur."* He captured her lips with his own. She traced his jaw with her finger. "What did you come up here for, my love?"

"Oh." He put her down and rubbed her belly. "I have a surprise for you."

"Oh?"

His chocolate-brown eyes glistened. "Your mother and sisters should be arriving today. They are coming to help with the baby."

Tears filled Mercy's eyes. As much as she loved Wyatt and enjoyed the life they were creating, she missed her mother and her family.

"I told them we'd be coming down in the fall, after the little one was born and it was the proper time for travel. They'll be staying with us for the rest of the summer and we'll travel together."

"Mother is willing to leave the ranch for that long?"

"Oui. Your father is hoping to come up for a week during the summer, as well."

Mercy's eyebrows rose. Father never left the ranch. "Really?"

"Yup, seems a grandchild is worth leaving the ranch in the care of Jack for a couple of weeks."

"Oh, dear. I need to start preparing the guest rooms."

"Shh." He took her in his arms. "Jason, his wife and I will take care of that. You take care of our little one." He caressed their child, and the babe obliged with a strong and steady series of kicks.

"I guess he's just as excited to meet his family as we are."

Wyatt knelt down in front of her and placed both hands on either side of the protruding bundle of joy.

"What do you think of the name Jonathan, if he's a boy? It means gift of God."

"I'd like that. Jonathan Stewart Darling. Stewart, for your dad."

Wyatt's eyes filled. "I like that, too."

"Now, what if he is a she?"

"Joanna?"

"Joanna Marie?"

"Yes, I'd like that." Wyatt rose with little hint of the slight hitch in his step from the attack over a year ago. So much had changed in their lives since that fateful day. The money had been returned with very little loss. The three men responsible had gone to prison, their lives ruined. But Mercy couldn't get over how the Lord had taken such a horrific event and turned it into the most incredible blessing of her life. "Wyatt, is it wrong to be thankful for that awful day?"

Wyatt smiled. "No, my love. God has a way of doing what is necessary to get us back on track with His plans for us. I am grateful and consider myself extremely blessed."

"Me, too." She reached out and embraced her husband again and kissed him on the lips. "I love you. You are *mon coeur*."

* * * * *

REQUEST YOUR FREE BOOKS!

2 FREE INSPIRATIONAL NOVELS
PLUS 2
FREE
MYSTERY GIFTS

Love Inspired™

YES! Please send me 2 FREE Love Inspired® novels and my 2 FREE mystery gifts (gifts are worth about $10). After receiving them, if I don't wish to receive any more books, I can return the shipping statement marked "cancel." If I don't cancel, I will receive 6 brand-new novels every month and be billed just $4.74 per book in the U.S. or $5.24 per book in Canada. That's a savings of at least 21% off the cover price. It's quite a bargain! Shipping and handling is just 50¢ per book in the U.S. and 75¢ per book in Canada.* I understand that accepting the 2 free books and gifts places me under no obligation to buy anything. I can always return a shipment and cancel at any time. Even if I never buy another book, the two free books and gifts are mine to keep forever.

105/305 IDN F49N

Name   (PLEASE PRINT)

Address   Apt. #

City   State/Prov.   Zip/Postal Code

Signature (if under 18, a parent or guardian must sign)

Mail to the **Harlequin® Reader Service:**
IN U.S.A.: P.O. Box 1867, Buffalo, NY 14240-1867
IN CANADA: P.O. Box 609, Fort Erie, Ontario L2A 5X3

**Are you a subscriber to Love Inspired books
and want to receive the larger-print edition?
Call 1-800-873-8635 or visit www.ReaderService.com.**

* Terms and prices subject to change without notice. Prices do not include applicable taxes. Sales tax applicable in N.Y. Canadian residents will be charged applicable taxes. Offer not valid in Quebec. This offer is limited to one order per household. Not valid for current subscribers to Love Inspired books. All orders subject to credit approval. Credit or debit balances in a customer's account(s) may be offset by any other outstanding balance owed by or to the customer. Please allow 4 to 6 weeks for delivery. Offer available while quantities last.

Your Privacy—The Harlequin® Reader Service is committed to protecting your privacy. Our Privacy Policy is available online at www.ReaderService.com or upon request from the Harlequin Reader Service.
We make a portion of our mailing list available to reputable third parties that offer products we believe may interest you. If you prefer that we not exchange your name with third parties, or if you wish to clarify or modify your communication preferences, please visit us at www.ReaderService.com/consumerchoice or write to us at Harlequin Reader Service Preference Service, P.O. Box 9062, Buffalo, NY 14269. Include your complete name and address.

LIDIR13R

REQUEST YOUR FREE BOOKS!

2 FREE INSPIRATIONAL NOVELS
PLUS 2
FREE
MYSTERY GIFTS

Love Inspired.

HISTORICAL

INSPIRATIONAL HISTORICAL ROMANCE

YES! Please send me 2 FREE Love Inspired® Historical novels and my 2 FREE mystery gifts (gifts are worth about $10). After receiving them, if I don't wish to receive any more books, I can return the shipping statement marked "cancel." If I don't cancel, I will receive 4 brand-new novels every month and be billed just $4.74 per book in the U.S. or $5.24 per book in Canada. That's a savings of at least 21% off the cover price. It's quite a bargain! Shipping and handling is just 50¢ per book in the U.S. and 75¢ per book in Canada.* I understand that accepting the 2 free books and gifts places me under no obligation to buy anything. I can always return a shipment and cancel at any time. Even if I never buy another book, the two free books and gifts are mine to keep forever.

102/302 IDN F5CY

Name	(PLEASE PRINT)
Address	Apt. #
City	State/Prov.	Zip/Postal Code

Signature (if under 18, a parent or guardian must sign)

Mail to the **Harlequin® Reader Service:**
IN U.S.A.: P.O. Box 1867, Buffalo, NY 14240-1867
IN CANADA: P.O. Box 609, Fort Erie, Ontario L2A 5X3

Want to try two free books from another series?
Call 1-800-873-8635 or visit www.ReaderService.com.

* Terms and prices subject to change without notice. Prices do not include applicable taxes. Sales tax applicable in N.Y. Canadian residents will be charged applicable taxes. Offer not valid in Quebec. This offer is limited to one order per household. Not valid for current subscribers to Love Inspired Historical books. All orders subject to credit approval. Credit or debit balances in a customer's account(s) may be offset by any other outstanding balance owed by or to the customer. Please allow 4 to 6 weeks for delivery. Offer available while quantities last.

Your Privacy—The Harlequin® Reader Service is committed to protecting your privacy. Our Privacy Policy is available online at www.ReaderService.com or upon request from the Harlequin Reader Service.

We make a portion of our mailing list available to reputable third parties that offer products we believe may interest you. If you prefer that we not exchange your name with third parties, or if you wish to clarify or modify your communication preferences, please visit us at www.ReaderService.com/consumerchoice or write to us at Harlequin Reader Service Preference Service, P.O. Box 9062, Buffalo, NY 14269. Include your complete name and address.

LIHDIR13R

REQUEST YOUR FREE BOOKS!
2 FREE WHOLESOME ROMANCE NOVELS
IN LARGER PRINT
PLUS 2
FREE
MYSTERY GIFTS

⁂⁂⁂⁂⁂⁂⁂⁂⁂⁂⁂⁂⁂⁂⁂⁂⁂⁂⁂

HEARTWARMING™

⁂⁂⁂⁂⁂⁂⁂⁂⁂⁂⁂⁂⁂⁂⁂⁂⁂⁂⁂

Wholesome, tender romances

YES! Please send me 2 FREE Harlequin® Heartwarming Larger-Print novels and my 2 FREE mystery gifts (gifts worth about $10). After receiving them, if I don't wish to receive any more books, I can return the shipping statement marked "cancel." If I don't cancel, I will receive 4 brand-new larger-print novels every month and be billed just $4.99 per book in the U.S. or $5.74 per book in Canada. That's a savings of at least 23% off the cover price. It's quite a bargain! Shipping and handling is just 50¢ per book in the U.S. and 75¢ per book in Canada.* I understand that accepting the 2 free books and gifts places me under no obligation to buy anything. I can always return a shipment and cancel at any time. Even if I never buy another book, the two free books and gifts are mine to keep forever.

161/361 IDN F47N

Name _____ (PLEASE PRINT) _____

Address _____ Apt. # _____

City _____ State/Prov. _____ Zip/Postal Code _____

Signature (if under 18, a parent or guardian must sign) _____

Mail to the **Harlequin® Reader Service:**
IN U.S.A.: P.O. Box 1867, Buffalo, NY 14240-1867
IN CANADA: P.O. Box 609, Fort Erie, Ontario L2A 5X3

* Terms and prices subject to change without notice. Prices do not include applicable taxes. Sales tax applicable in N.Y. Canadian residents will be charged applicable taxes. Offer not valid in Quebec. This offer is limited to one order per household. Not valid for current subscribers to Harlequin Heartwarming larger-print books. All orders subject to credit approval. Credit or debit balances in a customer's account(s) may be offset by any other outstanding balance owed by or to the customer. Please allow 4 to 6 weeks for delivery. Offer available while quantities last.

Your Privacy—The Harlequin® Reader Service is committed to protecting your privacy. Our Privacy Policy is available online at www.ReaderService.com or upon request from the Harlequin Reader Service.

We make a portion of our mailing list available to reputable third parties that offer products we believe may interest you. If you prefer that we not exchange your name with third parties, or if you wish to clarify or modify your communication preferences, please visit us at www.ReaderService.com/consumerschoice or write to us at Harlequin Reader Service Preference Service, P.O. Box 9062, Buffalo, NY 14269. Include your complete name and address.

HWDIR13R